WORLD OF IMPOSSIBLE THINGS

BOOK 5 · CURSE OF THE EMBER

TED DEKKER & H.R. HUTZEL

ISBN (Paperback Edition): 979-8-9888509-3-9

Also Available in the World of Impossible Things trilogy:

Legend of the Flames (Book Four)
ISBN: 979-8-9888509-2-2 (Paperback Edition)

Treasure Beyond World's End (Book Six)
ISBN: 979-8-9888509-4-6 (Paperback Edition)

Available in the Journey to Impossible Places trilogy:

The Fall (Book One)
ISBN: 979-8-9865173-3-9 (Paperback Edition)

The Great Divide (Book Two)
ISBN: 979-8-9865173-4-6 (Paperback Edition)

Redemption (Book Three)
ISBN: 979-8-9865173-5-3 (Paperback Edition)

Published by:

Scripturo
350 E. Royal Lane, Suite 150
Irving, TX 75039

Cover art and design by Manuel Preitano

Printed in China

The Impossible Places Series

Journey to Impossible Places

BOOK 1
The Fall
BOOK 2
The Great Divide
BOOK 3
Redemption

World of Impossible Things

BOOK 4
Legend of the Flames
BOOK 5
Curse of the Ember
BOOK 6
Treasure Beyond World's End

CHAPTER ONE

Raven

MICHAEL STOOD on the shore of the tiny island, staring at the barnacle-covered lighthouse that glistened in the morning light. He peered up at the darkened windows, knowing the top of the towering structure was empty. He and Rusty had investigated it yesterday after being sucked into the dome and making landfall. As Michael had feared, Tyler beat them to the first flame, extinguished it, and took the ember with him.

Eighteen hours had passed since the decrepit schooner was sucked into the swirling grey mass. Once it was inside, the storm and whirlpool had calmed, leaving Michael, Brynn, Rusty, and their crew stranded on a black, glasslike sea, the island with the lighthouse looming ominously in the center.

They'd sailed around the tiny landmass several times, searching for a way out of the dome. But the rounded structure sealed them in. Despite the protests of the crew, Rusty had tried to sail through the dome, saying it appeared to be made only of clouds.

But those clouds had nearly electrocuted them.

Fiery jolts of electricity had flared through their bodies as Rusty attempted to pass through the barrier. Their ship had hardly penetrated it when everyone aboard, including Winny and Rusty's cat, Penelope, began screeching.

They'd abandoned the task after four painful attempts and made camp on the shore of the island at nightfall. Rusty had spent the evening seated by his first mate, Jimmy, heads bowed together in deep conversation, Michael guessed strategizing a way out of the dome.

Even more surprising than finding himself stranded on an island—again—was the moment Brynn had joined Michael near the fire. She didn't say much, but it was the closest she'd ever sat to him.

As the sailors had dispersed to retire for the night, Rusty finally joined Michael and said, "In all the legends of the Divine Flames, never has there been a tale about someone succeeding in extinguishing them to harness their power. It's always been lore: douse the flame and harvest the embers. Clearly you were right, lad. A dark presence has penetrated Raven, and in extinguishing the flame, they've cursed these waters.

We can't breach the barrier with the ship. We'll have to find another way off this island."

Michael hadn't slept much that night, Rusty's words echoing in his mind.

We'll have to find another way off this island.

Memories of his first time stranded on an island had swirled in his mind, dredging up feelings of guilt for how he treated his brother, leaving him with an even more determined resolve to rescue Charlie.

If he could.

Brynn came to stand beside him and shielded her eyes against the morning light. Winny perched on her shoulder. She followed Michael's gaze and stared up at the lighthouse.

"A few members of the crew suggested cannons," she said.

"Cannons?" Michael asked.

"To fire at the dome. Don't worry, Rusty shut the idea down right away."

Michael sighed. "Good. If Lumina taught me one thing, it's that you can't fight darkness with more darkness."

Brynn smirked.

"What?" he asked.

She shrugged. "Just sounds like something the Sage would say."

Michael felt a grin tug at his lips. "Well that's nice to

hear. Because I feel like I've completely failed the Sage on this mission."

"It's always darkest before the dawn," Brynn said. "I still believe in you."

Michael's eyes widened.

"What?" Brynn demanded.

"That's the nicest thing you've said to me—ever."

She rolled her eyes.

"And *still*?" Michael asked. "You *still* believe in me? Does that mean you've believed in me all along? Even while you were hating me?"

She scoffed. "Don't read into things. I'm stranded on an island with you. You're the only Prince of Lumina around. Who else is going to save us? Besides, if I die here, you might be my last friend in the world."

Michael's jaw nearly dropped.

"Stop looking at me like that."

"I can't help it. You called me friend."

She folded her arms over her chest. "Don't push your luck. I can take it back."

Michael held up his hands. "Not pushing." He chuckled under his breath, feeling his stomach flip as he watched her smile.

"All right, Prince of Lumina, so you've been stranded on an island before. Cannons are out; sailing through the dome isn't an option; how do we get out of here?"

Winny squawked. "Follow the light."

Brynn reached into her pouch and pulled out a piece of dried fruit for the bird.

"He likes to repeat everything the Sage says," she explained to Michael. "I'm still trying to teach him a few phrases of my own, but he usually just ends up counting instead. She shook her head. "He's such a weird bird. Ow!"

Winny clenched Brynn's braid in his beak and pulled.

"That's not nice!" She pulled her hair from his mouth. "No treat for you." She put the fruit back into her pouch.

Winny screeched.

"As I was saying"—Brynn glared at the parrot— "any ideas for how we can get out of here?"

Michael stared at the lighthouse. "Not really." He pressed his lips together, thinking.

Rusty joined them. "Well, lad, the crew is looking to you."

Michael swallowed. "Looking to me?"

"Aye. Yer the boy who made the magical words appear on the map after all."

A weight settled on Michael's shoulders, then his chest.

"We're looking to you to get us out of this dome."

Rusty's words drifted through his mind, pushing past the fog of guilt.

"The map," Michael said. "Let me see the map."

Rusty pulled the rolled parchment from his pocket. "What do you have in mind?"

Michael unrolled it. "Maybe the riddle has a clue for how we can get out of here."

Rusty raised his red eyebrows. "Now that's an idea, lad," he said with a hint of hope.

Brynn took two corners of the map and helped Michael spread it out.

"Look!" she said, indicating an *X* on the far edge of the map.

"Whoa," Michael breathed.

Rusty's dark-brown eyes widened. "The coordinates to the second flame." He tapped the map with his thick finger. "Lad, this is . . . This is extraordinary. In all my years of questing, I never seen any hint to the location of the second flame."

"Michael, look!" Brynn said with excitement, nodding to the map, where illuminated words appeared.

Rusty inched back. "Mother Ocean, it's happening again!"

Michael read aloud.

"Through writhing seas you must prevail,
And heavy downpours you must sail.

"Beyond the queen's ferocious hive,

Bestow her treasure to survive.
Subdue her and the seas shall still,
Permitting those who dare and will
Divide the veil of deepest blue
To find the flame that burns with truth.
Shine, shine, O light, shine,
Through darkness to the flame divine."

His voice trailed off.

"It doesn't seem to have any hints for how we get off this island," Brynn said.

Rusty shook his head. "It's a riddle for the second flame. It has no use for us so long as we're marooned." The old sealord's shoulders slumped.

"Through darkness to the flame divine." Michael repeated the last line, then stared at Winny. "Through darkness to the flame divine . . . Follow the light."

The parrot straightened and flapped his wings. "Follow the light!" he squawked.

The Sage's words came rushing back.

The light is in you, and it will be your guide. Trust it, follow it. It shall never lead you astray.

"We have to search the island," Michael finally said.

"Fer what?" Rusty asked.

"The light," Michael said.

"The flame is gone, lad. We've already searched the lighthouse."

"Not that light," Michael said. "*The* light."

Rusty arched an eyebrow, but Brynn nodded.

"He's right," she said. "We have to search for *the* light."

Rusty mumbled, "This is why I don't have children," then louder said, "Yer not making any sense, lad."

Michael looked to Brynn. "The Sage told us to follow the light. I don't know what that'll look like here on this island, but if we can find it . . ." He turned and stared at the dark-gray stormy swirls that entrapped them. "It will lead us through the darkness." Facing Rusty and Brynn, he said, "We'll divide up the crew into groups of two and spread out to search for anything remotely luminous or shiny. The light is here. It's always with us, and it will be our guide."

✦✦✦

A couple hours later, Michael trekked across the small island, Brynn following close behind. So far, the only glowing object they'd seen was the obscured sunlight that penetrated the dome.

"This place gives me the creeps," Brynn said.

Michael glanced at her. Sweat beaded her fair skin. She pushed loose tendrils of fiery-red hair away from her face.

"This place gives me déjà vu," he said.

"Day-juh what?" Brynn scanned the sky, keeping her eyes trained on Winny, who flew.

"It reminds me of the island I was stranded on with Charlie and the rest of the kids from the orphanage."

"The island with the portal to Lumina?"

"Right." Michael nodded, then paused.

"What is it?"

He stepped through the dense vegetation into a clearing. Brynn followed.

He pointed across the open space. "Look."

Brynn followed his gaze to a black, gnarled tree that grew up the side of a rocky cliff. "I've never seen a tree like that before."

"I have," Michael said. "On the other island. The one with the portal to Lumina."

Her eyes widened.

Michael jogged across the clearing, Brynn close on his heels. They stopped beneath the leafless canopy of twisted black branches, then rounded the massive trunk.

"What are we looking for?" Brynn asked.

Michael swallowed, then lifted his hand. He pressed his palm against the cool stone of the cliff. The rock groaned as a doorway opened.

Brynn jumped back.

"We're looking for this." Michael grinned, then stepped inside.

Brynn's shoulder brushed his as she walked beside him. "It's pitch-black in here."

Michael heard a subtle quiver in her voice. His eyes adjusted.

"Not pitch-black," he said. "Look."

A dim yellow light flickered ahead, then approached.

Brynn gasped. "It's a solarfly!"

A smile pulled at Michael's lips. He stepped deeper into the cavern, rounding a corner. The rock opened into a brilliantly lit room.

"Not *a* solarfly," Michael said. "Hundreds of solar-flies." He chuckled. "*This* is how we'll get off the island."

The walls of the cavern flickered with yellow light as the glowing butterflies pulsed their wings.

"I wonder how they got here." He said under his breath. "I thought they existed only in Lumina."

But even as he said it, he remembered Charlie saw them before they'd ever traveled to their homeland.

A sudden wave of guilt returned as he remembered standing in a cavern nearly identical to this one. Recalled the moment he'd smashed one of the rare glowing insects, then threatened to end Charlie's life.

Michael hadn't known they were brothers then.

He stifled a shudder at the memory of the darkness he'd allowed to control him.

"Well, Prince of Lumina." Wonder filled Brynn's

voice. "If the solarflies are from your home, perhaps you called them here." She paused and glanced at him. The yellow glow warmed her face. "How will you get them to follow you out of this cave?"

Memories of his brother swirled in Michael's mind. He drifted back to the moment they'd liberated Lumina, then saved their friends on the island. Thousands of solarflies had appeared then.

"They're not going to follow me," he said. "We're going to follow them."

✦ ✦ ✦

Michael and Brynn raced through the last few feet of forest and broke through to the beach, following a swarm of glowing butterflies. Rusty and the crew had already returned from their search and froze when they saw the luminous cloud. Michael's chest heaved as he stopped to watch the swarm hover over the black glasslike sea, then come to rest on the deck and mast of their ship. One of the butterflies drifted away from the group and floated toward the dome's wall a half mile away from the shore.

Rusty approached, eyes glued to the glowing insects. "In all my years," he muttered. "In all my travels . . . I've never seen—"

"Look!" Brynn cut him off, pointing toward the lone solarfly.

The glowing insect brushed the swirling mass of clouds, then disappeared through it.

Brynn gasped. "It went through!"

Michael's heart stuttered as he stared at the spot where it had vanished.

Several seconds later, it reappeared through the dome.

The corners of Brynn's lips tugged upward.

"Are you thinking what I'm thinking?" he asked.

She grinned. "I sure am, Prince of Lumina."

"Everyone, get on the ship!" Michael shouted.

The crew hurried about the beach, dousing fires and packing the few supplies they'd brought to shore. They took turns using a rowboat to travel from the beach back to the ship. Once aboard, Rusty began barking commands. His first mate, Jimmy, at his side, helped command the crew.

"Raise the sails!" Rusty shouted.

"There's not enough wind," Jimmy protested.

"Aye," Rusty smirked. "But we'll make our own. Ain't that right, lad?"

Michael nodded, watching as the sails lifted and opened. The solarflies drifted into the air, then filled the canvases, pulsing their glowing wings.

The sails billowed out, then caught the breeze.

Rusty slapped his thigh and laughed.

Brynn gripped Michael's arm and squeezed. "You did it!"

"Don't get too excited. We still have to make it through this dome."

She stood beside him, Winny on her shoulder. "Follow the light!" The parrot squawked once again.

"Let's hope this works." Michael watched as the bow of the ship cut through the black sea and raced toward the barrier.

Swirling gray clouds loomed in front them, flickering with lightning at their approach.

Michael swallowed. In their previous attempts to cut through the dome, they hadn't been moving this fast. The wind created by the butterflies pulled them through water with heart-pounding momentum. There was no stopping it. If the dome was going to shock them at this speed, it would kill them.

He clenched his hands into fists, watching a wild-eyed Rusty stare up at the encroaching stormy wall.

The bow of the schooner pierced the dome.

The glow of the butterflies swelled, casting light over every inch of the ship.

Brynn grabbed Michael's hand. He glanced at her

from the corner of his eye. Her expression revealed that she didn't realize she'd reached for him. Despite the fear that swelled in his gut, a smile pulled at Michael's lips.

He held his breath.

The schooner sliced through the barrier, revealing brilliant daylight and blue seas on the other side.

The crew erupted with cheers.

Brynn glanced down at their joined hands and quickly released Michael's fingers.

He cleared his throat, then tucked his hands into his pockets.

Rusty appeared at Michael's side, leaving Jimmy at the helm. He stood beside the two kids, joining them as they watched the swarm of solarflies lift off the sails and drift off into the horizon.

"I can't believe it," the old sealord mumbled. He turned to stare at Michael. "Are you some kind of magician, lad?"

"Not at all," Michael said, holding Brynn's stare. "Just someone who follows the light."

Rusty nodded. "Well, this light you follow clearly has great power. Let's hope it leads us to the next flame—and before your friend reaches it." He held out his hand. "Let me see that map again."

Michael passed it to him, watching as Rusty unrolled it and scanned the coordinates.

"This here's at least a five-day's journey. If we move fast," he added. His brow furrowed. "And if we don't run into trouble."

Michael saw Rusty's lips move as he read the riddle silently. "And it sure sounds like trouble will be waiting for us." He rolled up the map and passed it back to Michael. "Looks like we might be needin' that golden lure after all."

CHAPTER TWO

Raven

TYLER CROSSED THE DECK of the *Black Dahlia* toward the bow, watching as one of the sailors vomited over the rail. He counted the man as the fourteenth crew member to fall ill since they'd fled the location of the first flame two days ago. He pulled the map from his pocket and traced the line from the first set of coordinates to the second, which had miraculously appeared after successfully retrieving the first flames.

He read the riddle silently, wondering at its meaning.

He silenced his mind and turned inward, listening for guidance from the dark voice who commanded him. He heard nothing but felt the tense presence of the Prince of Chaos. Reaching his hand under the collar of his shirt, he touched the cool metal dome in his chest. A swell of pride flooded his body.

Footsteps approached behind him. Tyler startled and dropped his hand.

Sealord Tomlin appeared at his side.

"This ember you call a treasure is cursing my crew," he growled, nodding to the sailor who hurled over the edge of the ship. "No one has touched it. We've followed your orders and yet it still poisons us." He fixed Tyler with a hardened stare. "This is not what you or your prince promised."

"They're just seasick," Tyler said, knowing it wasn't true. Not only had the majority of the crew fallen ill, but they were also going mad, losing their minds.

Tomlin scoffed. "These men and women are the finest sailors in all of Raven. They don't get seasick." He peered over Tyler's shoulder at the map. "We've been sailing two days with a dwindling crew. The *Black Dahlia* can easily cover the rest of the distance in another two days. Three if we hit foul weather. But at this rate, my crew won't last more than a day."

The Prince of Chaos hissed in Tyler's mind.

He crossed his arms over his chest and faced Tomlin. "What are you suggesting?" Tyler asked.

"I'm not *suggesting* anything," Tomlin growled. "I'm telling you to cast that ember into the sea, or I'm turning this ship around."

Rage flared inside Tyler, and he knew it wasn't only his own.

"No way," he said. "Do you know what kind of power that thing holds?" Tyler pictured the strange metal orb that encased the ember. He and Tomlin had agreed to keep it locked away inside the captain's quarters, where the crew wouldn't be tempted to touch it.

"The only power that thing holds is the power to curse and kill. You said so yourself. Which is why my crew and I have avoided it like the plague. And yet it seems a plague has still stricken us."

"I'm not getting rid of it." Tyler glared. "You want it gone, then you pick it up and toss it overboard yourself."

Tomlin's lips pressed into a tight line. "I'm turning this ship around."

No! The Prince of Chaos shouted in Tyler's mind.

"No!" Tyler repeated.

"You may have led us to the flame, boy, but I don't take my orders from a child. If we're to continue on this fool's treasure quest, then I need a cure for my crew. If the wind favors us, the *Black Dahlia* can reach Isla Sordes in just over a day." He tapped the map. "It'll be pushing it for the crew, but there's a medicine woman on that island. She has a cure for any curse the sea can hurl."

Don't lisssten to him. Keep presssing forward.

"No." Tyler stated. "Isla Sordes is in the wrong direction. We keep moving forward. We must extinguish the second flame."

"It was not a question," Tomlin said.

The Prince of Chaos murmured silent curses. A familiar sense of failure washed over Tyler.

"I won't let you down," he said under his breath to the prince, knowing that failure would be certain if their entire crew died at sea.

You'd better not.

"What was that?" Tomlin asked.

"Nothing," Tyler said.

"Just as I thought." Tomlin turned. "Commodore, set our course for Isla Sordes."

Commodore Beric, who'd been standing at a distance, approached. "Isla Sordes? Are you sure? We'll die if we go there."

"We have no other choice, Beric. Do as commanded."

The commodore hesitated, then said, "Yes, sir." He strode toward the helm, where Lieutenant Commander Eddard navigated the ship.

A wave of uncertainty washed over Tyler. "We'll die if we go there?" he asked, repeating the commodore's words. "What does that mean?"

Another crew member rushed to the edge of the ship and hurled the contents of her stomach into the sea. Tomlin's eyes snapped to her.

"I've made many enemies in my lifetime," Tomlin said. "Most of them can be found on Isla Sordes. But as I said, we have no other choice. We either die on land or die at sea." His lips twitched. "The sea can be a harsh mistress. I'll take my chances with my enemies."

Chapter Three

Earth

SARAH WATCHED as a man in a white lab coat removed a blood pressure cuff from her arm and began packing up his equipment. He'd checked her blood pressure twice because it was a little high the first time.

Which was to be expected after having been questioned by military personnel.

And tested like lab rats for the past two hours.

"All normal," he said, glancing between Sarah and Milo. He faced Mr. Abbott who'd been hovering in the corner of the bedroom where the physician's assistant had been running his tests.

"Even her blood pressure?" Mr. Abbott asked.

"Yes. They're healthy children." A slight crease formed on the man's forehead. "Everything about them seems perfectly normal." He shouldered his bag of equipment. "We'll have the blood results back shortly, but based on their physicals, I suspect their lab work will be as normal as the rest of them. I'll let you two get some rest," he said to Sarah and Milo. "You've had a busy day."

The door clicked closed behind him.

Sarah sighed. "I think the doctor is disappointed."

"What makes you say that?" Mr. Abbott asked, taking a seat at the end of the bed.

Milo perched on the other bed across the room, fidgeting with the gauze pad in the crook of his elbow. "Because we're not aliens."

Sarah rolled her eyes.

"You heard the doctor," Milo said. "We're *normal*. He said it like it was a disease."

Mr. Abbott chuckled. "Well, I for one am glad you're normal and healthy." He grinned. "And not aliens."

"Boring," Milo said in a singsong tone.

"He's right," Sarah said. "They were hoping to find an explanation as to why we could go through the barrier and touch the Anomaly."

She recalled the exhilarating moment of crossing the invisible barricade that had prevented anyone else from coming within a half mile of the dome.

"Well, of course they were," Mr. Abbott said. "But the three of us in this room knew they weren't going to find anything."

"It's because we've been to the island before," Milo interjected.

"I understand," Mr. Abbott said, as if everything that had unfolded over the past few days was as normal as Sarah's and Milo's physicals. "I am curious, though. Why was I able to step foot on the island?"

"Because we took you there," Milo explained. "But that's what made the island angry. That's why it put up a barrier to keep everyone else out."

"That's just a theory," Sarah said.

"Do you have a different theory?" Mr. Abbott asked.

She folded her hands in her lap and stared at her intertwined fingers, squeezing them tighter than she meant to.

"I don't know," she mumbled.

"It's fine. We don't have to talk about it anymore." Mr. Abbott glanced from child to child. "You two caused quite a stir." He ran a hand through his graying hair. "I have to say, in all my years, with all my connections and business dealings, I don't think I've achieved anything close to the publicity the two of you had today." He winked at Sarah. "You're practically famous."

She swallowed. "I know you're trying to make me feel better, but it's not helping."

"How famous?" Milo asked.

"The whole world watched you touch a dome that

not even a battleship can approach. That makes you a very hot topic."

"Like superheroes," Milo said with a smirk.

"An enigma at the least." He looked away, frowning. "But that's not our concern."

"Exactly," Sarah said. "We have to figure out how to save Charlie."

"Yes," Mr. Abbott said. "But even more we have to figure out why the dome is expanding?"

"The island can do a lot worse than expand," Sarah said.

"Maybe, but it's now being viewed as a threat. A weapon even."

"A weapon?" Milo said.

Mr. Abbott looked at him. "The dome could destroy whatever it touches. Its expansion is now only a few feet per hour, but their concern is that if they can't stop it, it could eventually grow large enough to reach land."

"Land?" Sarah said. "That's a long way off."

Mr. Abbott nodded. "This private island is the closest, so it would reach us first. It's still a long way off, but it's not stopping. And its rate of expansion could increase. For all they know, the Anomaly could swallow the whole world."

"No way," Milo said. He cocked his head. "Really?"

"The military always looks at worse case scenarios.

Nothing they've tried has had any impact on it. They know it's a dome that is sitting on top of the water and not a sphere, but submarines can't approach underwater because the forcefield extends to the bottom of the ocean."

"Submarines?" Milo exclaimed. "That's pretty cool."

"Every piece of technology the world has is pointed at the dome. And not just American." Mr. Abbott sighed. "To say that we have a major problem on our hands is a gross understatement."

"And I'm telling you, Charlie is the key," Sarah said.

"Maybe," Mr. Abbott said. "I'm going to step out into the hall and return a few phone calls. I received a voice mail from one of the lab techs they sent to the ranch to test the other kids who've been to the island. Guess what?"

"What?" Sarah asked.

"Unfortunately, they're all normal too." He shrugged. "Man, did I ever get fooled. Here I thought I'd adopted all of these extraordinary children just to find out they're the plain old boring kind."

That finally pulled a smile from Sarah.

"There she is," Mr. Abbott said, then kissed her forehead. He stood and started for the door. "Yup, just another boring adventure with my two normal kids. I'll check on you shortly." He disappeared down the hall.

Milo joined Sarah on her bed. "You know that guy who came in while they were drawing our blood?"

Sarah nodded. "The guy who was talking to Mr. Abbott?"

"Yeah. I heard him ask if they could run more tests on Charlie."

Sarah's eyes widened. "What did Mr. Abbott say?"

"He insisted they don't do anything that could harm him."

"They better not," Sarah said. "Either way, they aren't going to find anything. They know nothing about forces from another world."

Milo ripped off the gauze pad and prodded the spot where they'd drawn his blood. "Do you think they could tell if we had alien blood?"

Sarah frowned. "I think you watch too much television."

Milo shrugged. "No, I've been to a magical island."

Sarah stared at him for a moment then flopped back onto a plush stack of throw pillows. "I'm exhausted. It feels like weeks have passed since we touched the dome. But it's only been hours."

Milo flopped back beside her and stared at the ceiling. "I know. Any new ideas? After all, you're the smart one."

"The smart one? You're the one who came up with

the plan to steal the Zodiac."

"Yeah," he said. "That was pretty good, wasn't it?"

"And you're the humble one," she said under her breath.

"What was that?"

"Nothing." She grinned to herself. "We need to find another way to get close to the dome. There's no way we'll get access to any kind of watercraft from here on out. They'll be watching us closely."

"And we need to figure out a way to get inside."

"Exactly." Sarah stared at the blades of the ceiling fan, following their lazy circles, her mind stuck on one thought.

After several silent minutes, Milo asked, "You awake?"

"Yeah."

"Whatcha thinking?"

"There's one idea I can't shake . . ."

"See. That's because you're the smart one. What's your idea? A way to get inside the dome?"

"Maybe . . ." Sarah pressed her lips together, thinking of the stories Charlie had told her about his time in Lumina. He'd mentioned an old man he met—the Sage—who helped him survive an impossible situation. Perhaps he could help Sarah and Milo too.

If she could just find a way to get to him. The only

way she knew to do that was through a portal that led to Lumina—a portal on the island currently shrouded by an electrocuting dome.

But there was one other detail. Charlie once mentioned that the Sage told him he'd been watching Charlie and Michael through a connection on earth. And Sarah felt confident she knew who that person was—the benefactor who arranged for them to go on a mission trip a month ago.

The mission trip that had led them to the island.

Before she could say anything to Milo, the door swung open. Mr. Abbott stepped into the room, holding his phone. A perplexed expression lingered on his face.

"I . . . I just got off a call . . ." he said. "I . . ." He stopped, staring at them both.

Sarah sat up straight. She'd never seen Mr. Abbott at a loss for words. "Is it Charlie?" she asked, fearing the worst.

Mr. Abbott glanced down at the phone in his hand, then back up at his children. "No," he said. "It's about the two of you."

Sarah and Milo exchanged glances.

Mr. Abbott tucked his phone into his pocket. "The president wants to see you."

CHAPTER FOUR

Raven

TYLER PEERED OVER THE EDGE of the *Black Dahlia* at the thick veil of mist that shrouded the harbor of Isla Sordes. Dense clouds blocked out the midday sun. He shifted from foot to foot, feeling the ominous weight of the threats that awaited them.

Lisssten closely, my son. Your captain has made many enemies here. Therefore, they're now your enemies and mine. Tomlin has already put us off course, and there is someone else here in Raven seeking the Divine Flames. We don't have the luxury of time. We must move quickly and, if necessary, make sacrifices to put us back on course.

"Someone else is going after the flames?"

Yesss. I believe you know him.

"Michael," Tyler growled under his breath.

As I said, listen closssely to my voice. Trust no one.

Michael nodded his agreement, then followed Sealord Tomlin, Commodore Beric, Lieutenant

Commander Eddard, and a very ill Lieutenant Ferran as they disembarked the ship.

"You should stay on the *Dahlia* with the rest of the crew," Tomlin said to Ferran.

The lieutenant wiped his sweaty, feverish brow and pursed his pale lips. "I will do no such thing. I won't abandon my admiral in the presence of his enemies. Besides, I want to be first in line for Esmerelda's cure. We've lost one crew member already. I won't be the second."

Tomlin gave a swift nod. "Keep your head down," he said to their small group. "We must move quickly. Though our entire crew is still on the ship, I don't feel confident in their abilities to defend it. Not in their current state." Tomlin's brow formed a hard, chiseled line. "It won't be long before he knows we're here."

"He?" Tyler asked.

"Sealord Damien Dutchman," Tomlin said. "I once stole something very precious from him. I also owe him a great debt." He cast a glance over his shoulder back at their ship. "Now, come," he said as he led them down the dock and onto the streets of Isla Sordes. "We mustn't waste any more time."

Mist withdrew as they proceeded, revealing a worn cobblestone street. Abandoned carts dotted the shoulder, interspersed with vagrants sipping from dark-tinted bottles. The scent of rotting trash mingled with the salty air and distinct whiff of ale. Laughter poured from the open doors of a tavern. A sailor stumbled out, his arm draped around the shoulders of a beautiful woman.

Tyler slammed into the shoulder of another sailor crossing the street.

"Watch where yer going!" The man spit at Tyler's boots.

Fire flared in Tyler's veins, but he gritted his teeth and kept moving. The sailor turned and scanned their group, arching an eyebrow, then turned from the tavern and scuttled off into the shadows of an alley.

Tomlin mumbled something, then louder said, "Don't make me regret bringing you to shore, boy."

After several more twists and turns down the misty streets of Isla Sordes, Tomlin led them through the front door of a shop marked with a fancy script that read *Apothecary*. A tiny brass bell dinged as they stepped inside.

A heavy herbal scent filled Tyler's nostrils. He breathed in the fragrant smell, grateful to be rid of the stench of the streets. His eyes scanned the shelves that lined the walls and the countless amber-colored vials and bottles filled with tinctures and salves.

A beaded curtain behind the counter parted as a

woman stepped through from a back room. She stiffened when her eyes landed on Tomlin. Her skin, nearly as dark as her hair, glistened in the warm lanternlight. She flicked her long black hair over her shoulder, then perched a hand on her narrow, corseted waist. A crimson red dress swept the ground as she stepped around the counter and narrowed her golden eyes.

"Tomlin . . . The last time you were here, you promised me I'd never see you again."

"What can I say?" Tomlin shrugged. "I'm not great at keeping promises."

The woman snorted. "This I already know." Her full lips curled into a sneer. "I've rid my heart of you once. If I have to do it again, I'll slit your throat."

"It's good to see you too, Esmerelda." Tomlin inclined his head toward her.

With the speed of a trained marksman, Esmerelda unsheathed a dagger from her waist and flung it. The knife sailed past Tomlin's head with inches to spare and got stuck in the wooden wall behind his head. He didn't even flinch, but a cruel smile parted his lips.

Commodore Beric rolled his eyes. "Must it always be like this with the two of you?" To Tyler he said, "Meet Esmerelda, the only woman to capture Tomlin's heart after his beloved wife passed." Beric scrutinized the couple with his gaze. "Their relationship is . . . interesting."

Esmerelda's smile met her eyes as she crossed the room to remove her dagger from the wall. Tomlin circled her like a shark.

Esmerelda grinned, then stepped behind the store counter once again. "To what do I owe this pleasure? Besides your broken promises."

Tomlin leaned his forearms on the counter. She mimicked his posture, their foreheads nearly touching.

Tomlin's expression turned serious. "I'm here with my crew and ship."

"*Your* ship?"

Tomlin waved her words away. "We're in the middle of job." He glanced over his shoulder at Tyler. "Under the command of a very powerful prince."

Esmerelda's eyes sparked. "Go on."

"My crew has fallen ill. Quite ill," he added.

Esmeralda straightened and backed away a step. "I hope you haven't brought us a plague."

"Not a plague—a curse."

"Which is so much better." Esmerelda wiped her hands on the skirt of her dress. "Tell me more of this curse. What caused it? Whose grave have you robbed this time?"

Tomlin lowered his voice. "My crew and I have a powerful object in our possession."

"Gold? Silver? You'll have to be more specific."

Tomlin cleared his throat. "One of the Three Divine Flames. The ember, in fact."

Esmerelda stared at him, then laughed.

"It's no joke," Tomlin said, straightening.

Esmerelda picked up a rag from behind the counter and began dusting a shelf. "You and your wild tales, Tomlin. Do you really expect me to believe you've gone chasing a legend?" She chuckled. "Well, that I can believe. But that you actually found it?" She scoffed. "Quit wasting my time."

A teenage girl appeared from the back room through the beaded curtain. "Miss Esmerelda, I have those tinctures packaged up for delivery. Shall I take them now?"

Esmerelda held up a hand, signaling her to wait.

"It's true," Tomlin said through gritted teeth. "Look at Ferran. Have you ever seen the man so pale?"

"Once," Esmerelda said with a glance over her shoulder. "After a long night at the tavern."

Tomlin growled. "I'm serious."

Esmerelda set down her dusting rag. "Fine. Your crew is sick, from what manner of curse it doesn't matter. I have nothing to cure imaginary illness caused by imaginary flames, but I have a remedy you can try. I read about it in my great grandmother's journals. I've never used it before, but it's said to cure even the strongest of sea curses. It's the best I can offer. Wait here."

The teenage girl followed her through the beaded curtain into the back room.

"This better not take long," Ferran said, dabbing at his forehead with a handkerchief. "I haven't eaten in a day and a half, and yet it still feels there's something to come up." He clenched his stomach.

Tyler slipped away from the group and wandered down an aisle of the shop, scanning the labels and contents of the amber-colored jars. He passed several familiar items: lavender, oregano, thyme, even thieves oil. They lined the shelves, intermingled with strange ingredients he'd never heard of: wolfsbane, lady's mantle, and bleeding tooth fungus. He stared past a vial of witch hazel to see a small terrarium filled with live frogs and, beside it, a jar with dried owls' feet.

He shook off a shiver and returned to the group, hoping he didn't fall ill like the rest of the crew. He wasn't about to drink a tincture made with any kind of bird's talons.

Tyler could feel the unsettled stir of the Prince of Chaos. The wait for Esmerelda's return felt long—too long. Every minute they stood in the apothecary was another minute Michael gained on the second flame.

Finally Esmerelda appeared carrying a brown paper

bag. She lifted a jar from the package, her eyes darting to the door, then to Tomlin.

"One teaspoon of this in your sailors' tea is all you should need." Her eyes shifted to the door again. "According to my grandmother, that is."

"I thought you said it was your great grandmother," Beric said.

"Oh yes, of course. My great grandmother." She returned the jar to the paper bag.

A bell dinged behind them, and Tyler turned to see Esmerelda's assistant enter from the front, a fierce-looking man behind her.

He stepped into the shop, his knee-high boots clomping heavily on the wooden floor. A long red coat draped his shoulders, and a curved scabbard hung from his belt.

"Damien Dutchmen," Tomlin sneered. He spun to pierce Esmerelda with his stare. "You betrayed me!"

She set the paper bag on the counter. "I'm just returning the favor. Besides, you're not the only one who owes the Dutchmen a debt." She stared past Tomlin toward the dark-haired, thin-eyed sealord. "We're even now?" she asked.

Sealord Damien tilted his head. "Your debts are paid. But yours, Lord Tomlin, are not."

Black leather gloves covered Sealord Damien's

hands, but they barely muffled his clap. Five sailors entered the shop. "Oh, Tomlin, Tomlin," he said in a mocking tone. "Such a fool to come back to this island. And in the very ship you stole from me. Tell me, how is my beautiful *Black Dahlia*?"

Tomlin clenched his jaw as one of Damien's sailors forced his arms behind his back and tied his wrists together. Another stepped behind Tyler, binding him with coarse rope. Within minutes the rest of Tomlin's men stood bound beside them.

"No need to answer," Sealord Damien sneered. "I shall see her soon enough." To his men, he said, "Take them to the dungeons. It's time for Tomlin to pay his debts."

CHAPTER FIVE

Raven

THE PENELOPE SLICED THROUGH the deep-blue waters, her sails taut with wind. Michael smiled as he breathed in the salty air and peeled an orange. Rusty had cautioned him and Brynn of the importance of eating as many fruits and vegetables as possible before the produce rotted and they had no access to the vitamin-rich foods.

Brynn appeared at his side with her own orange.

"No scurvy for us," he said.

A smile flickered on Brynn's lips as she peeled the fruit, then offered the first segment to Winny. She popped a piece into her own mouth and chewed. "I just spoke to Rusty. We're coming up on the coordinates of the second flame. Have you figured out the riddle yet?"

Michael handed her his orange to hold and pulled the map from his pocket. He unrolled it and read aloud.

"Through writhing seas you must prevail,

And heavy downpours you must sail.
Beyond the queen's ferocious hive,
Bestow her treasure to survive.
Subdue her and the seas shall still,
Permitting those who dare and will
Divide the veil of deepest blue
To find the flame that burns with truth.
Shine, shine, O light, shine,
Through darkness to the flame divine."

He rolled it up, tucked it away, then took his orange from Brynn. "After Rusty read the riddle, he mentioned the golden lure."

She shared another bite with Winny. "What's a golden lure?"

Michael swallowed. "He said it had something to do with sea dragons."

"Sea dragons?" Brynn tossed the orange peel over the rail of the ship. "That doesn't sound good."

Michael finished his own orange. "It doesn't sound real. I mean, c'mon. Dragons?"

Brynn shrugged. "Rusty thought the flames were a legend, and they're clearly real. Maybe there's something to this sea dragon thing."

"Good point," Michael said, noting that the schooner had slowed and the crew had fallen deathly silent.

Rusty appeared at their side and pointed to the

horizon. "Do you see that sliver of land in the distance?" he asked in a hushed tone.

Michael and Brynn followed the point of his finger.

"That there is our destination," he said, keeping his voice low.

Excitement swelled in Michael's gut. "I don't see any other ships. Do you? Maybe we beat Tyler here."

"It's possible, but yer friend could also be on the other side. We'll know as we get closer. We'll keep our distance as we make our approach, circle the island, and make sure we're alone before making landfall." His eyes widened. "There! Do you see that flicker?"

Michael searched the horizon, then saw a flash of light.

"The flame!" Rusty said in an excited hush.

"Why are you whispering?" Michael asked, keeping his own voice low.

"Beyond the queen's ferocious hive," Rusty said. "Bestow her treasure to survive."

"The riddle," Michael said.

"Aye. There's only one kind of queen you'll encounter upon the open waters . . ."

In unison, both Michael and Rusty said, "Sea dragons."

Rusty nodded. "Good thing I brought the golden lure."

"How does it work?" Michael asked.

"Well, the last time I used one—"

"The last time?" Michael interrupted. "You mean you've actually seen a dragon before? They're real?"

"Quite real, lad. And as the riddle indicates, very ferocious. 'Tis why we must be quiet. We don't want to draw more attention to ourselves than we already have. Your riddle suggests there's a hive nearby. As for the golden lure . . ." He paused, tilting his head. "Do you hear that?"

Michael shook his head. "Hear what?"

Brynn held up a hand and shushed him. "I hear it too."

Michael fell silent and listened.

Something thumped the hull of the ship. Near silence followed, the gentle lap of waves against the schooner the only sound.

Rusty lowered his voice even more. "We need to get to shore as quickly as—"

The ocean erupted behind them. A six-foot-long monster leapt from the water and launched itself onto the deck of the schooner.

Brynn screamed and backed away, crashing into Michael as Winny shrieked.

Thicker than a man's thigh and lined with razor-sharp spines, the sea dragon flopped on the deck, flapping the winglike fins it presumably used to launch itself out of the water. It swung its long neck wide, fangs bared, hissing. Another thump hit the hull. Then another creature, bigger than the first, sprang onto the ship.

"Harpoons!" Rusty shouted as a third sea dragon propelled itself from the sea onto the *Penelope*. It swiped its spiny iridescent-blue tail, striking Brynn in the calf and slicing open her leg. Blood seeped from the wound, darkening her pants with a blackish-red stain.

"Get her back!" Rusty commanded. "There's poison in their spines! And their bite!"

Brynn crouched on the deck, trembling hands gripping her calf. Winny, still perched on her shoulder, beat his wings and uttered ear-piercing cries.

Michael dropped down beside her as he heard the fourth and fifth sea dragons land on the ship.

Chaos erupted, but Michael narrowed his focus to Brynn and her leg.

Blood seeped through her fingertips where she clutched the wound. "It's—it's not—it's not that bad," she said through chattering teeth. Her normally fair skin was whiter than the sails of the most pristine clipper.

Michael peeled her hands from the wound. "No, it's bad. And you're going into shock."

Blood puddled around her thin body.

He tried to help her to her feet, but she immediately collapsed into his arms.

"Get her outta here, lad!" Rusty shouted.

Michael spun to see the red-haired sealord slice off the head of one of the dragons. The body flopped around the deck for a few beats, then stilled.

Two more flew over the rails of the ship, teeth bared.

Michael spun back to Brynn and thrust his hand out at Winny. "Winny, up!"

The bird didn't hesitate and scaled his arm to his shoulder.

Squatting, Michael lifted Brynn into his arms and carried her cooling body to the captain's quarters. He slammed the door closed. Squawking, Winny fluttered off his shoulder and perched on a beam.

Michael set Brynn down on the threadbare mattress where Rusty slept, then ripped off his shirt, tore it into strips, and tied it around her calf just above the wound. After checking that the makeshift tourniquet was tight enough, he searched through Rusty's belongings until he found a knife and cut away the bottom portion of Brynn's right pant leg.

A necrotic spiderweb of veins surrounded the wound.

"Poison," he whispered.

He peered up into her hollow eyes. Her body began to seize.

"It's poison," he said louder. "I don't know what to do."

Brynn's eyes rolled back until only the whites showed. She clenched her teeth, then gasped. "Ju—ju—just—hold me."

Michael dropped onto the mattress beside her, lifted her upper body, and gripped her against his chest, holding her tight as wave after wave of bone-wracking seizures rolled through her body.

The chaos outside fell silent. Seconds later, Rusty burst through the door to the captain's quarters. His eyes fell on Brynn, who trembled uncontrollably in Michael's grip.

Without a word, he rushed to a wooden chest in the corner of the small room. He flung it open, ripping out sweater after threadbare sweater until he pulled out a bundled blanket. He unrolled it to reveal a growler-sized jug. Uncorking it, he carried it across the room.

"Hold her head back," he commanded.

Michael obeyed, watching as the sealord poured a green liquid into Brynn's trembling mouth. She coughed and sputtered, but Rusty kept pouring. After several good glugs, he drenched her wound.

"She'll be fine," he said in a clipped tone. "But the others might not. I'll be back."

Curse of the Ember

He rushed out of his quarters with the jug.

After several agonizingly long minutes, the seizing slowed, then ceased. A faint amount of color returned to Brynn's cheeks. She lay in Michael's arms, exhausted.

After several more minutes, Rusty appeared in the doorway, carrying the jug. He tipped it upside down. "Empty," he said. "I only have one more jug of the antidote." He wiped his sweaty brow and flopped onto the end of the mattress, eyes scanning Brynn, then Michael. "You did good, lad. The tourniquet was a good call. Probably the only thing that stopped the poison from getting to her heart. It moves quickly." He breathed heavily. His dark-brown eyes scanned Michael. "Perhaps you're a hero after all."

Michael shifted, adjusting Brynn in his arms. "The rest of the crew?" he asked.

Rusty sighed. "I don't know how it's possible, but everyone is alive."

Brynn stirred.

"What happened out there?" Michael asked.

"Exactly what I was trying to avoid," Rusty said. "We sailed right into their nest."

"What do you mean?"

"Sea dragons are hive creatures. They have a queen, who's usually quite docile. The rest are males and hellbent on protecting her."

52

"Like honeybees?" Michael asked.

"Honeybees are female," Brynn uttered.

"Aye. Most of them, except for the drones. But yes, similar to honeybees. And just like honeybees, if you can capture the queen dragon, you can control the entire hive. Unlike honeybees, if you kill the queen dragon, the entire hive dies with her. Instantly."

"Instantly?" Michael asked.

Rusty nodded. "They can't live without her."

Michael pushed the sweaty strands of hair from Brynn's face, then helped her sit up.

"So what do we do?" Michael asked. "We have to get past them to get to the flame."

A wry smile tugged at Rusty's bearded lips. "Fortunately, we have our golden lure." His eyebrows arched. "C'mon, lad. It's time to go fishing."

CHAPTER SIX

Earth

SARAH'S KNEES BOUNCED up and down. She clenched her hands together in her lap, silently counting as she sucked in one steadying breath after another. She glanced at Milo, seated beside her on the couch in the White House's Oval Office.

"How did we get here?" she asked.

Milo's mouth smacked as he loudly chewed the piece of gum he'd been chomping since their private flight into Reagan National Airport.

"Limo, remember?"

Sarah sighed. Keeping her voice low, she said, "Of course I remember. I mean how in the world are we the ones sitting in the Oval Office right now about to meet the president?"

Before Milo could respond, Mr. Abbott, who'd been standing behind the couch, placed his hands on Sarah's shoulders and gave her a reassuring squeeze.

"Relax," he said. "Everything's going to be just fine."

"Right," Sarah mumbled under her breath. "Relax."

But at what point in the strange chain of events could she relax?

When her best friend had fallen into a coma?

When two of her adopted siblings had gone missing?

When a massive dome had erupted from the ocean, cutting her off from the only hope of rescuing her friends?

Perhaps she was supposed to relax while being ushered by Secret Service agents from the airport into the backseat of a blacked-out limousine?

Or when Milo had questioned their mysterious suited driver about his occupation as one of the Men in Black?

Or while being scrutinized by security and forced to empty every single skort pocket before being ushered into the president's office through what looked like a hidden door?

"I don't think I can relax until this is over," she finally said.

Mr. Abbott chuckled, then released her shoulders.

Sarah scanned the rounded room. A second couch sat opposite theirs, a thin coffee table between the two. To her right sat the iconic Resolute desk backlit by three massive windows. Thick drapes stretched from ceiling to floor, dwarfing the two Secret Service agents who stood beside them.

Painted portraits of former presidents surrounded a fireplace on the left. Side tables on either side of the hearth showcased two bust sculptures, one of Martin Luther King, Jr. and another person Sarah didn't recognize.

A door across from them swung inward. Sarah froze, her knees ceasing their bounce. She hadn't noticed the door until it opened. It blended into the wall like the one they'd entered.

The president stepped into the Oval Office.

Sarah wondered if she should stand up. Bow Perhaps? Or maybe curtsey?

Fortunately the president made the decision for her.

"Welcome to the White House," he said with a warm smile. "No need to get up. I'm going to join you."

Two men dressed in black suits entered behind him. One whispered into his sleeve.

Milo leaned closer to Sarah and said, "More Men in Black. I bet they're going to wipe our memories before we leave."

The president smirked. "I promise to leave your memories intact." He glanced past them to Mr. Abbott, who walked around from behind the couch.

"Mr. President, it's a pleasure to see you." He held out his hand in greeting.

The president shook his hand. "Please, Richard, call me Andy."

A smile tugged at Mr. Abbott's lips. "Only if you call me Richie."

Before Sarah could discern what was happening, the president had pulled Mr. Abbott into a bear hug, and they were smacking each other on the back.

"Richie, my friend, how the heck are you?"

Sarah and Milo exchanged glances as the two men made brief small talk, then joined the kids on the couches. Mr. Abbott took a seat on the other side of Milo while the president sat across from them.

Sarah cleared her throat. "You guys know each other?"

Mr. Abbott smirked. "Oh didn't I ever tell you about my friend from Harvard, Andrew Taylor—better known as President Andrew Taylor?"

Sarah stared at him, then shook her head.

"We met on the men's lacrosse team and roomed together our senior year."

"That's right," the president said. "We've stayed in touch over the years, and Richie was a major supporter in my campaign. He's as loyal as they come."

"He is," Sarah said proudly, thinking of the way Mr.

Abbott had believed her and Milo when they'd told him their insane story about the island.

"And these must be your lovely children," the president said. "Two of them, that is. You always wanted a big family."

Mr. Abbott beamed. "This is Sarah and Milo. They're great kids."

"And brave," the president added. "I've seen the footage of your little excursion." He raised his eyebrows. "And I have some questions, which is why I brought you here. To start, why did you approach the Anomaly? It was almost as if you knew you'd be able to get close to it."

Sarah swallowed, her throat dry. Mr. Abbott had prepared them for this moment on the flight to DC, saying she needed to be honest with the president and that he was someone she could trust.

"Sir—I mean, Mr. President, with all due respect, I'm not sure you'll believe me."

The president leaned forward, resting his forearms on his knees. "Young lady, I'm the president of the United States. I know our nation's greatest secrets, even the unbelievable ones. Why don't you try me?" he said with a warm smile.

Milo leaned in. "So you know about Area 51? And Roswell? And the aliens?"

The president shifted his attention to Milo. "Young

man, I have no idea what you're referring to." The president winked.

Milo gasped and leaned back against the couch. "I knew it," he said under his breath.

"Now, which one of you would like to start filling me in?"

Sarah's eyes darted from the president to Mr. Abbott to the Secret Service agents.

The president followed her gaze. "You can trust them. Everything you say in this room is confidential."

"Go on," Mr. Abbott said.

Sarah sucked in a shaky breath. "I can't believe I'm about to tell you this," she said.

And then she did.

She told him about the island and how she and her nine adopted siblings had crashed there. She filled him in on every crazy detail about the mysterious landmass: the purple fruit, the vanishing plane, the disappearance of Charlie and Michael, and the horrific effects the island had inflicted on each of them, leading to the tragic death of Maxine.

The president leaned back when she'd finished. His face revealed nothing. "An island," he said. "And only those who have been there can see it?"

"And those who are called to it," Milo added.

"Right," the president said. He faced Mr. Abbott. "But, Richie, you said you stood on this island."

"I did."

"How is that possible?"

"Because we took him there," Milo said. "But we shouldn't have. It made the island angry." He blew a bubble with his gum, then popped it with a loud snap.

"That's just a theory," Sarah said, realizing their story sounded even crazier with Milo's commentary.

"Theories are good," the president said, watching curiously as Milo leaned back and propped his feet on the coffee table. "You have a different one, Sarah?"

She glared at Milo and motioned for him to move his feet. He ignored her, snapping his gum once again.

"I think it has something to do with Michael and Tyler's disappearance. And Charlie's coma."

"You said that Charlie and Michael disappeared the first time you were on the island. And Charlie is the one who's in a coma?"

Sarah nodded. She wasn't sure the president was actually buying their story, but at least he was listening.

He cleared his throat. "So what happened to him and Michael the first time? They disappeared, but where did they go?"

Sarah thought about saying that it wasn't her secret to tell, but instead she said, "There's a lot about that island that we don't understand. Which is why we're so concerned about our friends."

The president exchanged glances with Mr. Abbott, who shrugged.

"I certainly don't understand it any better than they do, Andy. Their story has stayed consistent. And we've all seen them penetrate the invisible barrier that prevented anyone else from getting within a half mile of that thing. Even the Navy couldn't breach it. I mean c'mon, Andy. They touched the dome."

"Felt like Jell-O," Milo interjected.

Mr. Abbott's voice tightened. "I watched that thing rise from the depths of sea. I believe the island is still there. And my boys are trapped."

The president stood and paced. "Richie, you know you're like family to me. So that makes your kids family too. I'll do everything in my power to help you get them back. But I have an entire nation to think about. The Chinese are issuing threats with the Russians who seem convinced it's some kind of weapon. A test of new technology gone wrong. I'm having trouble convincing them otherwise. Both countries are sending aircraft carriers and battleships. There's a whole lot at stake here, you must understand that."

He stopped, staring at his desk, looking truly concerned.

"The world is watching, and that thing is growing," he said. "I was hoping you could shed some light on how to penetrate the dome, but it seems you're as much in the dark as we are. If we can't make some progress soon, we'll have to take more extreme measures. We have to either get into that dome or destroy it."

Sarah shifted, tucking her hands under her legs. She didn't like the sound of that. Not at all.

The president returned to the couch across from Sarah and leaned forward. He lowered his voice. "The world may be looking to me, Sarah, but I'm looking to the two of you. Are you sure you have no idea how we can penetrate the dome?"

Sarah's heart hammered against her chest. "I—I don't," she said. "But I think I know someone who might." She glanced between the president and Mr. Abbott. "They call themselves the Benefactor."

CHAPTER SEVEN

Raven

LiEUTENANT FERRAN'S COUGH echoed through the jail cell. Tyler watched as the pale man groaned and leaned his head back against the damp stone wall. He hacked up a greenish phlegm and spit into a bucket in the corner, then slid to the ground, shaking.

"Based on the symptoms the rest of the crew has experienced," Ferran panted, "I'm only a few hours away from fever dreams and hallucinations." He clutched his stomach. "And perhaps seconds away from emptying my stomach again."

"I'll get us out of here," Tomlin said. "And get you that remedy, even if I have to burn that apothecary to the ground. I won't let you die."

"Meanwhile"—Lieutenant Commander Eddard winced—"stay close to that bucket."

Ferran nodded, then curled up beside it on the cold floor.

Tyler stared through the bars of their shared cell, watching as a figure approached through the dim torchlight.

Commodore Beric jumped to his feet, reaching for his sword, then remembered it had been confiscated before they were thrown into the prison.

Sealord Damien appeared, draped in shadow.

"You were brave to come back here after what you did to me, Tomlin. Did you think I'd forget the debts you owe me? And my precious ship you stole?"

"Of course not." Tomlin sneered. "All you have are your debts."

Sealord Damien's jaw muscles twitched. "And yours have come due. It's time to pay up."

Tomlin stepped closer to the bars. "Why pay with treasures when I can offer you the thing you truly want?"

Damien arched an eyebrow.

"A chance at my life," Tomlin said. *"Duelo a muerte."*

"Admiral, no!" Beric shouted.

Damien's lips curled into a sneer. "Live by the sea; die by the sword."

"What's happening?" Tyler asked.

Tomlin smoothed his hands over his jacket. "A duel to settle my debts. They'll be paid with my life or my debtor's. Live by the sea; die by the sword. But it shall be I who lives to sail another day."

Damien's eyes thinned to slits. "You're a good swordsman, Tomlin. But I've always been better. You'll say hello to the devils of the deep for me, yes?" He turned and strode away. "After all, you'll be meeting them soon."

We have a problem, the Prince of Chaos said. *We need Tomlin alive. You can't allow this to happen.*

Tyler turned away from the admiral and his men and whispered into the darkness. "What should I do?"

A long moment passed before the Prince of Chaos spoke again. *You must speak to Damien. We need to convince him there's something he desires more than the debt Tomlin owes him.* A sinister chuckle echoed in Tyler's mind. *We don't need Sealord Tomlin. We just need a sealord.*

✦ ✦ ✦

Hours passed. Tyler sat in the far corner of the jail cell, formulating a plan in his mind while watching Tomlin pace and listening to Beric try to convince him not to enter a death duel with Damien. The sounds of Ferran's dry heaving served as the backdrop.

We're running out of time, the Prince of Chaos said.

Tyler stood. "I have a plan," he whispered. He strode across the cell to the barred door, putting on a show of clutching his stomach and groaning. "Guard," he called out in a miserable tone. "Guard!"

A man approached from down the hall.

"Whatdaya want?"

"I'm going to be sick," Tyler said. "Please, I need a toilet."

"There's a bucket in the corner. That's your toilet."

"The bucket's full," Tyler said, glancing back at Ferran. "Unless you want a mess to clean up, I suggest you take me to another bucket." Tyler made a gulping sound, then covered his mouth.

The guard's eyes widened. He ripped a set of keys from his belt, unlocked the door, then ushered Tyler out. "Move quickly. Down the hall." The guard locked the cell, then followed Tyler, keeping a wary distance.

"Take a left at the end of the hall."

Tyler obeyed, then slowed when he was out of earshot of Tomlin and his men. He turned.

"Oh, no," the guard said, backing away. "Is it happening? Control yourself, boy. Hold it in. We're almost there!"

Tyler kept his voice low. "I need to see the Dutchman."

The guard's face cycled through expressions of disgust, surprise, then anger. "You're not sick."

Tyler thrust his hands into his pockets. "Not at all. I feel great, actually."

"And what's a boy like you want with the Dutchman? Here to beg for your life?"

Tyler straightened and took a step closer to the guard. The pudgy man inched back, still afraid of getting vomit on his boots.

"I serve a powerful prince. A wealthy prince," Tyler added. "And my prince has business to conduct with the Dutchman. If you help me, I'll make sure you're rewarded for your cooperation. If you stand in my way . . . Well, I'll make sure you're rewarded for your actions."

The guard's lips curled with a sneer. "Fine," he said. "I'll take you to the Dutchman." He shrugged. "Doesn't much matter to me. Cuz if the Dutchman doesn't like what you have to say, then it'll be you who suffers." He stepped in front of Tyler. "Follow me."

The guard led Tyler through the prison halls, then directed him out onto the dark streets. Night had already fallen on the island, casting shadows deeper than Tyler had ever seen. They didn't have to travel far to the tavern where the guard guided him through a door behind the bar and up a set of stairs. He paused at the top and rapped his knuckles against the thick wood of another door. Several seconds passed before it cracked open. Someone peeked out, then swung the door wide.

Tyler stared at the striking young woman in the doorway. Her black hair, pulled back from her face in a sleek braid, framed creamy skin and dark narrow eyes. She wore fitted black pants and boots with a white blouse neatly tucked in at the waist. She paused when she saw Tyler.

"We're busy," she said.

The guard dipped his head. "Forgive me, m'lady, but the boy wishes to see the Dutchman."

"Who is it?" Tyler heard a familiar voice ask from inside the small apartment.

The young woman stepped aside, allowing both the guard and Tyler to pass.

Sealord Damien Dutchman sat at a small desk, leaning back in his chair, boots propped up on the tabletop.

When he saw Tyler, he swung his legs down and sat up straight in his chair. "You. You're one of Tomlin's crew." His eyes flashed to the guard. "Why isn't he locked up with the rest of them?"

The guard started to speak, but Tyler cut him off. "I'm not a member of Tomlin's crew. He's a member of mine."

Sealord Damien interlaced his fingers and rested his hands on the desk. Tyler noted he still wore the black leather gloves. "Then it's from you I should collect my debts?"

Tyler folded his arms over his chest, feeling the rolled parchment of the map he'd concealed inside the lining of his jacket before disembarking the *Black Dahlia*. "Nah, you can still collect your debts from Tomlin."

Damien's dark eyes glinted. "You'd betray a man as powerful as Admiral Tomlin?"

Tyler's mind drifted to the vial of seawater and blood and the oath he'd made with Tomlin.

"Tomlin and I have an arrangement. If he's unable to fulfill his end of the deal, then I'm free to do as I wish."

"And what is it you wish to do?"

Tyler strode across the room and took a seat in the chair across from Damien. He propped his boots up on the desk as he'd seen the sealord do.

"I wish to continue my mission—my prince's mission, to be specific."

"And which prince do you serve?" Damien scanned him, his thin eyes lingering on Tyler's boots. "Surely not the royal crown."

"The prince I serve isn't from here. He's far more powerful than any man in Raven."

The young woman in the room scoffed, taking a seat beside the fireplace on the wall opposite Damien. A red coat that matched the Dutchman's draped across the back of her seat.

"More powerful than any woman in Raven too," Tyler added.

She rolled her eyes.

Damien's chair creaked as he shifted. "You're boring me. Get to your point."

Tyler swung his feet to the ground and leaned across the desk. "My prince has sent me on a mission to capture the Three Divine Flames. Sealord Tomlin was accompanying me on my quest, but it's become clear that he's a liability to this mission. I'm not a sailor, so I need a sealord, but it doesn't have to be Tomlin. And before you tell me that these flames are just a myth, I have one already. I've extinguished the first flame and have the ember to prove it."

Damien's lips pursed. He glanced at the young woman seated beside the hearth.

"Join me," Tyler said. "Do as you wish with Tomlin. The *Black Dahlia* and her crew are yours. Help me finish my quest, and I'll make sure Tomlin's reward goes to you. But we need to move quickly," he added. "There's someone else after the flames. We must reach the second one before he does."

Damien's face remained placid, but Tyler could tell his wheels turned beneath the surface.

"You have questions, clearly," Tyler said. "I'm happy to answer them, but first, let me put your doubts to rest. Let me show you the ember. It's on the Dahlia." Tyler stood. "I can show it to you now."

"This is a trap," the young woman said. "Surely the

crew is waiting to slit your throat the moment you board."

"The crew is ill," Tyler said. "They're no threat. And me?" He grinned. "What can I do? I'm just a boy."

Damien's lips flickered with a fake smile.

Tyler reached into his jacket.

The young woman jumped to her feet, shoving back her chair. She crossed the room in seconds, dagger drawn and aimed at Tyler.

Damien stilled her with a signal of his hand.

"It's just a map," Tyler said, reaching into the slit he'd cut into the lining of his jacket. He pulled out the roll of parchment. The young woman's shoulders dropped, but she came to stand behind Damien, still clutching the dagger.

Tyler spread the map across Damien's desk. "Here's where we found the first flame," he said, indicating the *X* on the map. "I solved the riddle, extinguished the flame, and secured the coordinates to the second." He tapped the second *X*. The young woman leaned in, studying the map over Damien's shoulder. "There's another riddle, and you'll need me to solve it." He lifted the map and returned it to his jacket.

"You have the first flame," Damien repeated.

Tyler nodded. "Come aboard, and let me show you. If you still don't trust me, then bring as many armed men—or women—as you'd like to protect you. I can assure you—"

"I don't need protection," Damien interrupted, pushing back from the desk. He stood. "I'm Sealord Damien Dutchman, rightful captain of the *Black Dahlia*, commander of the Dutchman's Fleet." He smoothed his hands over the breast of his red jacket. "Now, take me to my ship."

✦ ✦ ✦

Tyler stood inside the captain's quarters on the *Black Dahlia*, watching as Damien strolled through the room, grazing his gloved hands over every surface.

"My beautiful, girl," he murmured. "Oh, how I've missed you." Wooden boards creaked beneath his feet as he passed the four-poster bed and strolled to the desk before a window covered with heavy curtains.

When Damien turned away, Tyler silently locked the door.

"It feels good to be reunited with her." Damien spun. "Now, where's this ember?"

Tyler stepped into the center of the room, pausing on a round rug. He pointed downward, then crouched, lifting the corner of the thick fabric. He felt along the floor for a loose board, pulled it up, then lifted a chest from below.

"Of course," Damien said.

Tyler placed the chest on top of the captain's desk. "Only problem is the chest is locked. And the guards took my key."

Damien reached into his pocket and produced a small keyring. He jangled it in front of Tyler's face.

Tyler watched as the sealord tried a few keys before finding the one that clicked in the lock. He slowly opened the chest.

Tyler held his breath.

Damien peered inside the wooden box. "There's nothing in here but a shiny ball. I've never seen a metal like this before, I'll give you that. But this is no treasure."

Tyler felt a rush of ice in his body, the chill emanating from the strange metal dome implanted in his chest.

Open the housing on the ember, the Prince of Chaos commanded. *Show him what's inside.*

Tyler pushed past him and lifted the metal orb from the chest, feeling the smooth surface until his fingers found the small key on its side. He twisted it, and the casing snapped open, revealing a pulsing round ember. The light was hypnotic, like glowing coals in the bottom of a campfire. Sealord Damien took a step closer.

"I can't believe it," he murmured. "It's real." He slipped off his gloves. Tyler's eyes lingered on the man's right hand. The ring and pinky fingers were missing.

He glanced down at the gloves Damien had set on top of the desk. The right one contained false fingers.

Ssstop him! The Prince of Chaos shouted in Tyler's mind.

He snapped his head up in time to see the sealord take another step closer. Before Tyler could say or do anything, Damien touched the ember.

No!

Tyler backed away, horrified at his own failure. He banged into a coat rack and spun, seeing one of Tomlin's jackets and a baldric with sword.

Light swelled in the captain's quarters, and when Tyler turned back toward Damien, the man crouched on the floor, clutching his right hand before his eyes, weeping.

He peered up at Tyler, flexing five fingers on his right hand.

"I'm healed!"

Fool!

"The legends are true," Damien said. "The Divine Flames hold the power to heal!" Damien picked up the ember and cupped it in his hands. "If their embers contain this much power, imagine what the flame itself can do. We must find a way to reignite it."

You've failed me!

Damien stood up. "And, yes, I will help you on your

quest. I must see all three of these flames." He stared at the glowing ember. Wonder filled his voice. "I want to bask in the light of their presence!" He laughed with joy.

"I'm sorry," Tyler mumbled under his breath. "I'm sorry, Father, I've failed you."

You are no longer fit to call me Father. My true ssson never would allow this to happen. You were supposed to show him the ember to convince him, not to heal him.

"I'm sorry. I'm so sorry. Please, I can fix this."

You can't fix this. He'll tell everyone about the power of the light in these flames.

"I'll tell him not to speak of it, threaten him, bribe him—anything."

There is nothing you can do.

"There has to be something!"

Damien glanced at Tyler for only a second, too enraptured with the ember and his healed hand to care about the mumbling boy.

There is only one way to sssolve this problem.

"Name it," Tyler said, lowering his voice. "I can do it."

You can't.

"I can. Please. Please don't abandon me. I can do better. I can *be* better. Just tell me. What do you need me to do?"

Silence answered his question. Then the voice spoke.

Do exactly as I sssay.

Another icy surge raced through Tyler's veins. The metal dome in his chest burned cold as the Prince of Chaos gave his command.

Tyler's mind fogged. Clarity abandoned him as he turned and removed Tomlin's sword from the baldric, following the silent orders of his prince.

Without a sound, Tyler unsheathed the weapon and approached Damien from behind.

He watched himself as if in a movie. As if from hovering above.

As if he were another person watching a friend about to make the biggest mistake of his life.

He wanted to scream at himself to stop.

But the dome in his chest pulsed with a chilling vibration, reminding Tyler of his connection to the Prince of Chaos, to the island, to the one who'd chosen him.

To the one he had chosen too.

He pointed the tip of the sword at the center of Damien's back and braced.

When the sealord turned, Tyler ran him through.

The ember slipped from Damien's hands and landed with a thud.

A thud like Maxine's body collapsing onto the sand.

The ember rolled across the floor and to the corner of the room.

The Dutchman gasped. A gurgling sound bubbled in the back of his throat. His eyes widened as his body slumped.

Tears streamed down Tyler's cheeks.

"I'm sorry," he said. "I didn't have a choice."

Damien sucked in a wet, labored breath. "You—always . . ." he wheezed. "You always have a—have a choice."

Life fled his eyes.

Then he was gone.

The full weight of the man's body fell onto the sword.

Tyler dropped it, staring at the body, his hands, the blood.

"No," he whispered. "No, no, no. What have I done?" His hands trembled. "What have I done?"

Sssilence! You did what had to be done. I'm proud of you, my ssson.

Bile crept up the back of Tyler's throat. He vomited.

Pull yourself together. Our work here isn't finished.

Tyler wiped his mouth with the back of his hand.

You can't leave this mess.

"Mess?" Tyler said. "He's a man. And I killed him!"

He was an obstacle. And you overcame it. Now, remove the sssword and clean it.

Tyler's body moved mechanically as he disassociated from the moment.

Now, listen to me carefully. This is the ssstory you

will tell: The ember killed Damien, just as you promised it would if someone touched it.

"The ember killed Damien," Tyler repeated, his voice hollow.

Pick it up.

Tyler crossed the room and retrieved the ember.

Now touch it to Damien's wound.

Tyler obeyed, watching as the opening sealed with clean flesh.

The ember cannot resurrect him. Only the flames can do that. The ember's powers, though still great, are dulled once the flame is extinguished. But at least now, the wound from the sword is gone.

"The ember killed Damien," Tyler mumbled.

That's right. Very good. Now, clean up. There must be no trace of what actually happened here.

"The ember killed Damien."

Tyler's mind fled his body, retreating from the horror and gruesome task at hand.

He moved swiftly, silently, the voice of the Prince of Chaos encouraging him at every step.

Good. That's it, my ssson. I'm ssso proud of you.

Time passed, but Tyler didn't know how long. Finally he finished cleaning and staging the scene.

There is one last thing to do.

Tyler's eyes landed on the black leather gloves still

on the captain's desk. He reached into the fingers of the right glove and removed the two wooden pegs that filled the sleeves, giving the appearance that Damien had all five of his fingers. The sealord didn't need them now, and Tyler had to hide what the ember had truly done. He tucked the pegs into his pocket and replaced the gloves on Damien's hands.

Well done. You've proven yourself worthy. Now, you must run and tell everyone what really happened here.

"The ember killed Damien," Tyler said in a robotic voice.

Yesss, the ember killed Damien. Now go!

Tyler's eyes swept the room one last time, ensuring he hadn't missed any details. He wiped the tears from his cheeks, then ran from the captain's quarters and into the night, screaming, "Help!"

CHAPTER EIGHT

Raven

A SLIVER OF DAWN PIERCED the thick clouds that shrouded Isla Sordes and warmed the deck of the *Black Dahlia*. Tyler stood leaning against the rail, watching Tomlin and Beric as they huddled together at a distance, heads bowed in deep conversation. A hollowness ached in his stomach, his bones. He wrapped his arms around himself, shivering despite the warm breeze.

Tomlin glanced over his shoulder, meeting Tyler's blank stare, then approached. Beric followed.

"It must've been rough to see what you saw last night."

Tyler straightened his shoulders, trying to appear stronger than he felt.

"I remember the first time I saw a dead body," Tomlin said, placing a warm hand on Tyler's shoulder. "You never forget the first."

An image of Maxine's face drifted through his mind.

"Now we know what your prince said is true. No one on this ship will go anywhere near that ember."

Beric eyed Tyler with a scrutinizing gaze. "Tell me again why the Dutchman dragged you onto this ship."

Tyler's eyes flickered to the harbor and the streets of Isla Sordes beyond.

"I told you. I was sick. And when the guard took me out to the bathroom, he started questioning me, asking me why I was here, what I was doing with Tomlin and his crew. When I mentioned the flames, he immediately took me the Dutchman."

Commodore Beric shook his head. "I still can't understand why you said anything about the flames." He narrowed his eyes as he spoke.

"He's a child, Beric. Let it go. Besides, it all worked out in our favor."

"I was sick," Tyler repeated. "I wasn't thinking clearly."

"Well, you seem to have recovered much quicker than the rest of the crew."

"Beric," Tomlin warned. "He took Esmerelda's remedy just like the rest of us. He'd only begun to show symptoms last night, so of course he recovered quickly. Was he foolish to open his mouth about the flames? Yes. But it led to the Dutchman's demise all the same."

Tyler's stomach flipped.

Tomlin's gaze drifted past Beric. A smile tugged at the admiral's lips.

Tyler turned to see Esmerelda climbing the stairs from below deck. "It seems every member of your crew should make a full recovery." She handed a small glass jar to Tomlin. "Extra," she said. "Should you run into any other curses on the open sea."

"How do I know it's not poison?" Tomlin asked in a teasing tone. "You've betrayed me once."

She stepped closer and wrapped her arms around his waist. "You betrayed me; I betrayed you. We're even now. I hope you'll think twice about double-crossing me again."

"Thank you for saving my crew."

She waved his words away. "Poor fools. It's not their fault their captain led them astray."

"I believe you mean their admiral." Tomlin pulled her arms from his waist and took her by the hand. "Now, dear lady, please allow me to escort you off my ship. I should hope to see you again when I pass through these waters on my return."

Esmerelda whispered something Tyler couldn't hear and followed Tomlin to the ramp where a familiar young woman in a red coat stood, a man behind her.

"Permission to come aboard, Admiral," the woman said.

Tomlin released Esmerelda's hand. "Permission granted."

The woman Tyler had seen in Sealord Damien's apartment strode up the ramp. Once aboard, Esmerelda hurried past her and down the dock, keeping her head low.

"Captain Nadia," Tomlin said, inclining his head.

"Admiral Tomlin Kingsbury."

"I'm sorry to hear the news of your father."

Tyler stiffened and stifled a gasp.

Nadia's eyes flickered to him, then back to Tomlin.

"You're not sorry, and neither am I. The Dutchman was a cruel man and a harsh father."

Tomlin folded his arms over his chest. "I have to say I'm surprised to hear you say so. You've always been a loyal captain in his fleet."

"And because of that loyalty I've now inherited his fleet."

"Ah," Tomlin said. "Raven's first sealady."

She scoffed, eyes flicking to Tyler once again. She held his stare, though she spoke to Tomlin. "How fortunate that my father agreed to a *duelo a muerte* shortly before his death. That's quite convenient for you. Your debts are paid with his blood."

Tyler swallowed, wondering how many seconds he had left before she told Tomlin what had really happened when Tyler went to visit the Dutchman.

"Fortunately for you, I'm as happy as the rest of Raven to be rid of him."

Tyler silently sighed his relief.

"Then I suppose you've come to collect his ship?" Tomlin said, straightening, as if bracing for a fight.

Nadia dragged her gaze away from Tyler to Tomlin. "*His* ship? Why, I thought the *Black Dahlia* belonged to you?" A smile twitched in the corners of her lips.

Tomlin dropped his shoulders. "It does," he said, dipping his head in silent thanks.

"I heard that your crew fell ill."

"All recovered now," Tomlin said. "Or at least well on their way."

"Very good. But I also heard you lost a man at sea." She turned to face the man she'd brought aboard. "Please accept my gift of one of Isla Sordes's finest sailors to fill the spot in your crew. A peace offering, if you will. As the new sealord of the Dutchman's Fleet, I plan to handle things differently than my father and form alliances rather than enemies."

"That's quite generous of you, but what's the catch?"

"No catch," Nadia said, turning to stroll back toward the ramp. "Your debts are paid; the *Dahlia* is yours, and your crew is complete. Which means our business here is finished, until I call upon you for a favor." She spun, an eyebrow raised.

"Or I need a favor from you?" Tomlin said with a sly grin.

"Favors are most certainly welcome within an alliance." Her lips parted with a full smile. "I trust this means you'll be on your way?"

"We'll have left Isla Sordes by midday."

She nodded. "Very well. Oh, and thank you for having your men deliver the Dutchman's body to the morgue. I saw him before coming here."

"Of course."

Nadia glanced at Tyler, then strode down the ramp.

"Well," Tomlin said, facing Commodore Beric. "I guess coming to Isla Sordes wasn't such a bad idea after all. We'll give the crew a couple more hours of rest. Then we set sail for the second flame."

Tyler watched the two men stroll down the deck toward the helm. His eyes drifted over the rail and glimpsed Nadia disappearing into the misty streets of Isla Sordes, her red coat billowing behind her.

CHAPTER NINE

Earth

SARAH WAITED in the same living room where she'd been questioned by military personnel, scientists, and other official-looking people she didn't recognize. She sucked in a deep breath, still trying to process how she'd gotten herself into this position, recalling what the president had said to her: she was the expert on the world's greatest mystery.

"No pressure," she whispered under her breath.

Yesterday, both Mr. Abbott and the president expressed great interest in Sarah's theory about the benefactor who'd arranged their mission trip gone wrong. The president had drilled both Sarah and Milo with questions about this mysterious person, but even Mr. Abbott knew very little of the woman, Adelaide Luken, whom he met at a charity event a couple of years ago. She'd impressed him. The brilliant businesswoman had inherited her father's wealth and company, then built multiple orphanages and schools in third-world countries across the globe. When she reached out to him to invite the children of Saint Francis's Boys and Girls Home to participate in a mission trip to Mexico, he thoroughly vetted her organization. His investigation raised no red flags. Adelaide seemed perfectly safe. So Mr. Abbott had agreed to the trip, not realizing it would lead to a plane crash involving his children and an event that would rattle the world.

Sarah had struggled to answer some of their questions because there was so much she didn't know herself, but they didn't have anything to lose by setting up a meeting with the mysterious woman.

Sarah stared at the open doorway across the living room, waiting for the benefactor to arrive.

From what she'd heard from Mr. Abbott, the president had summoned Adelaide Luken straight to Washington, DC, before sending her here. She'd most certainly received a grueling round of questioning—and re-questioning. Sarah hoped she hadn't caused too much trouble for the woman.

She also hoped Adelaide could provide some answers. Specifically, how Sarah could get in touch with the Sage. She sighed. It felt like a long shot. But it was her only hope.

Footsteps approached the room.

Sarah straightened her shoulders and smoothed her short black hair.

Milo strolled through the door.

Sarah slumped.

"Wow," he said. "Don't look so happy to see me." He joined her on the ivory linen sofa.

"I'm just nervous," Sarah said. "The benefactor is an important and busy woman."

Milo shrugged. "She agreed to come here. It was her choice."

"Yes, but Mr. Abbott said she doesn't know any more than we do. What if she's angry with us? What if she's coming here just to warn two children about making wild assumptions, and—"

"Whoa. Slow down. You're going off the deep end. Breathe."

Sarah sucked in a shaky breath. "I can't do this anymore, Milo. I can't! It's too much pressure. I feel like I'm going crazy. And I can't stop thinking about Charlie. What if he dies?"

"You're spiraling," Milo said.

"I know!" Her voice cracked. "Why aren't you? We're both having the same experience!"

"No we're not," Milo said.

She lowered her voice. "What do you mean?"

Milo shifted to face her.

"We're both experiencing the same events, but we're not having the same experience." When he saw her confused expression, he continued. "I like to think of my life as a movie or a TV show."

"No surprises there," Sarah mumbled.

He smirked. "You do it too," he added.

"No, I don't."

"Sure you do. Everyone does. Most people just don't realize it."

Sarah considered his words, then said, "Well, the last couple of months have certainly felt like a movie."

He nodded. "The difference between you and me is that when I picture my life as a movie, I imagine myself as the hero." He paused. "You see yourself as the victim."

Sarah swallowed. "You might be right."

"I am right," he said with a grin. "Heroes are always right."

She rolled her eyes, but his words pulled a smile from her.

The click of heels sounded down the hall. Seconds later, Mr. Abbott appeared in the doorway, a blonde woman beside him.

"Sarah, Milo, this is Adelaide Luken."

"Hello!" The woman greeted them in a warm tone. Her bright floral dress swept the floor as she crossed the room and held out her hand.

Sarah stood to greet the petite woman who stood only a couple of inches taller than her. Sarah guessed her to be in her late forties, though she looked much younger.

"The lieutenant wants to speak to me," Mr. Abbott said. "So you three take a few minutes to get to know one another, and I'll join you shortly." He retreated down the hall.

The benefactor took a seat in the armchair across from Sarah and Milo. "It's nice to meet you both," she said. "Richard said you wanted to speak to me. And after my surprise visit with the president, I thought it best to have this conversation in person." She winked.

"You're not mad?" Sarah asked.

"Mad? About what?" Genuine confusion marked her face.

"Oh," Sarah said. "Never mind." She searched for words. "We want to talk to you about the dome and the island inside it."

Adelaide shifted to the edge of her seat.

Sarah glanced at the doorway, wondering how much time she had before Mr. Abbott returned. "Specifically, we want to talk to you about Lumina."

"Ah, yes. Lumina. I suppose Charlie and Michael told you about that mystical world?"

Sarah nodded. "Charlie also told us about the Sage."

She decided to use bold words, though she was certain of nothing. "We know you're connected to him, that you're his eyes and ears in this world."

Adelaide raised her eyebrows. "I suppose I am."

"I was right?" Sarah breathed. "I was right! We need to talk to him," she blurted. "Michael has gone missing. Along with Tyler, one of the other kids from the orphanage. And Charlie is in a coma. We think it's all connected." She winced realizing how ridiculous it all sounded. "Look, all we know is that Michael and Tyler went back to the island, and now they're trapped inside the dome. We need to do something! The Sage is the only one who can help us. And you. You can help." She sucked in a gulp of air.

Adelaide let out a slow breath. "Oh dear. This is going to be disappointing."

Sarah's stomach clenched.

"First, let me start by saying that's a lot for two young people to process. Heck, it's a lot for adults to process. I'm glad you reached out to me. You both are very brave."

Milo elbowed Sarah in the ribs.

"And the disappointing part?" Sarah asked.

Adelaide offered a consolatory smile. "I'm afraid neither I nor the Sage will be much help."

The benefactor's words snuffed out Sarah's last ember of hope. "Why not?"

"Oh, where to begin." Adelaide leaned back and crossed her legs. "When I was a young girl, I began having dreams of a mystical world called Lumina. The dreams were so vivid, I began to think of them as real. Every night when I fell asleep, it felt as if I were settling in to read a book or watch a movie. Lumina had an entire history and lore: a tale of a dark force that deceived a man and used him to usher darkness into the land."

"The Sovereign," Sarah said, recalling the tale Charlie and Michael had shared upon their return.

"Yes." Adelaide nodded. "And the Sovereign had two sons: one named Michael, one named Charles." She paused. "When I turned thirteen, the dreams began to change. No longer did I just receive images, pictures, and histories of the world . . . I began to see the image of a man who came and spoke to me directly. You know him as the Sage."

Sarah shifted.

"Over the course of my teenage years, the Sage began preparing me for a mission. He explained that a time difference existed between the worlds, and in the future, these twin boys from Lumina would be sent through a portal to Earth. I was to watch over them and, if necessary, send them back to Lumina one day.

"Shortly after I turned thirty-five, I learned the boys had arrived on Earth. I kept close watch over them from afar. Of course, I'm assuming you can fill in the details. A little over a month ago, I was told to arrange for the twins to board a plane bound for the Gulf of Mexico. The rest is history."

Sarah chewed the inside of her lip. "So the Sage appears to you in dreams? Does that mean you can talk to him?"

"I'm afraid that's the disappointing part. Communication is one way."

"Aw, man," Milo said. "I was hoping you could just create a portal to go see him."

Adelaide laughed. "Of course I can't do that."

"But that's what Tyler did," Milo said. "He created a portal to the island."

Adelaide tilted her head. "Tyler can't create a portal."

"Why not?" Sarah asked.

"Because Tyler isn't a portal walker."

"What's a portal walker?"

"A portal walker is someone who has been through a portal to another world and come back. The Sage explained it to me once."

"Like Charlie," Sarah said.

"And Michael," Milo added. "That's how Tyler did it. He used Michael."

"But what about the Sage?" Sarah asked. "He can create portals, right? Surely he must know what's happened to Charlie and Michael."

Adelaide shifted, glanced over her shoulder at the door, then continued. "Look, I only know what I've learned through my dreams. You and I could never fully comprehend this, but there are entire histories and timelines of countless worlds that exist. Wars and battles, territories, and agreements . . . All I know is the Sage doesn't have jurisdiction on Earth. He's a powerful man, but he has no power here. Just as we have our own limitations, he has his. Which is why he needed me to get those boys on the island in the first place."

"So it's hopeless," Sarah said, feeling the full weight of their situation.

"Nothing is ever hopeless," Adelaide said. "While Charlie and Michael have their limitations as well, they also have great power. As do the two of you. And so long as the light still rules—which it does—the darkness can never snuff it out. I'm terribly sorry you're going through this. And that I can't be of further help."

"But what can we do?" Sarah asked, feeling more like a victim than ever before. "I'm terrified of what will happen to them . . . What will happen to the world . . ."

Adelaide stood. "I wish I could offer you more answers. But the only thing I can think to extend to you is this bit of wisdom: you can't fight fear with fear. You must choose another way." She strolled toward the door.

"I have full confidence in Charlie and Michael—and in you, Sarah and Milo. The four of you will find another way. I do believe the fate of the world may depend on it."

With a simple smile and a nod she disappeared through the doorway.

CHAPTER TEN

Raven

THE DAY AFTER THE SEA DRAGONS attacked their ship, Michael watched Rusty put the finishing touches on a woven fishing trap big enough to hold an adult man. He threaded copper wire in and out of the basketlike weave, a bundle of cane, cable, and cord on the deck beside him.

Yesterday, immediately after administering the dragon-poison antidote to the affected crew, Rusty had ordered Jimmy to push off from the coordinates of the second flame. Otherwise, they'd be sitting directly on top of the hive.

Michael had busied himself late into the night by helping Rusty construct the trap to catch the queen, but that didn't stop him from checking on Brynn at least once every hour. By morning, she'd hobbled out of the captain's quarters to find both Michael and Rusty asleep on the deck beside the half-finished trap. The three of them had spent the rest of the day weaving cane and copper.

"The female sea dragons—the queens—are biologically quite different from the males," Rusty explained as his deft fingers worked. "They're a tad smaller, roughly five feet or so, while the males average six to eight feet. Though the older ones can grow to ten feet in length if they live long enough." He paused to wipe sweat from his forehead.

"How long do they live?" Brynn asked, standing beside Michael with her weight on one leg.

"A few hundred years if they're lucky."

"Whoa." Brynn wrapped her arms around her waist.

Michael stared at the bandage around her right calf.

Rusty began unwrapping a large brown paper parcel beside him. "You can tell how old they are by counting the rings on their tails. The males are a deep-blue color on the top, turquoise on the bottom, with silvery rings on their hind ends. No one knows how long the females can live. They don't have rings." He lifted a foot-long golden object from the parcel. It reminded Michael of a boat propeller. Sunlight glinted off the paddlelike edges as it spun.

"I've heard some sailors say the females are ageless," Rusty continued. "I don't know if I believe that, but," he shrugged, "no rings. So who can say how old they are?"

Michael's eyes traced the oblong object. "That's the golden lure? It doesn't look like anything. I've only been fishing a couple of times, but the lures always looked like an insect or bait. How does this attract the queen?"

"Good question, lad." Rusty affixed the lure to the inside of the trap, hanging it as far back into the basket as possible. "The queen dragons are attracted to gold."

"Why?" Brynn asked, picking up Penelope as she slinked past her on the deck.

Winny uttered a loud cry, beat his wings, then glided from Brynn's shoulder to Michael's.

"Gold is a mineral," Rusty explained. "And a necessary mineral for the female sea dragons. It's essential for laying eggs. She's fiendishly attracted to it. Which is why ships at sea are often a target. Over the centuries, these creatures have learned that where there be sailors, there be gold. They've caused more than one shipwreck. Which is why I asked Jimmy to push off from the coordinates. The males will viciously attack a ship for the chance to secure a meal for their queen."

Michael glanced back at the gray-haired man at the helm.

"That thing must have cost you a fortune," Brynn said. "That's a lot of gold."

"Aye," Rusty said, avoiding her gaze.

"Rusty?" Brynn's tone held suspicion. "How exactly did you pay for this?"

"How I conduct my business is none of yer business."

Michael saw a hint of the old curmudgeon they'd first met on Isla Pobre.

"It's okay, Brynn," Michael said. "Let it go."

Rusty sighed. "No, it's fine. It's just . . ." He glanced away. "I've never been a wealthy man. You've seen my home. Any other time I've needed a golden lure, I leveraged myself heavily to get it." When he saw the confusion on the kids' faces, he said, "I went into deep debt to get them. Or made agreements with men I never should have." Rusty dusted off his hands and stood. "But after years of seeking the flames and failing—and losing everything in the process—my word isn't what it used to be. No one will give me a loan these days. But I had a small amount of cash saved up from my marine mechanic days. It wasn't enough, so I . . ."

"So you what?" Brynn asked.

"I sold my home and my boat yard. I sold everything I had."

Michael furrowed his brow. "So you're saying—"

"I'm saying I've got nuthin' to go home to, lad. Not even a home. I went all in. I bought the field and the pearl."

Michael's mind drifted back to that moment inside Rusty's shack.

"The Three Divine Flames are like a treasure hidden in a field," Michael said, recalling the legend Rusty had shared with them. "When a man found them, he hid them again, and then in his joy went and sold all he had and bought that field."

Rusty's eyes misted. A subtle rasp filled his voice as he said, "The Three Divine Flames are like a merchant looking for fine pearls. When he found one of great value, he went away and sold everything he had and bought it."

Michael shook his head. "But why? Why would you give up everything for this?"

A smile pulled at Rusty's bearded lips. "Because I believe in you, lad. I've spent my entire life chasin' the flames—what I believe to be the greatest treasure of all. And when you believe something that deeply, you go all in. There's no turning back for me."

The weight of Rusty's words barreled into Michael.

The sealord slapped him on the back and quickly changed the subject. "So we use gold to lure the queen in." He pointed to the trap. "And copper to disorient her. It's quite toxic to the females. She's only aggressive if you stand in between her and her gold."

Jimmy left the helm to join them. Rusty motioned for him to help as he tied a line to the trap and tossed it over the starboard edge of the ship. The buoyant cane Rusty had used to weave the basket kept the trap afloat while the copper and gold weighed it down just enough to sink below the waves. He let out the line until the trap bobbed about thirty feet away.

"The sun'll be setting soon," Rusty said, "and dusk is the perfect time to hunt. The males are less active later in the day, which is to our advantage. And the lighting is key."

Michael tried to shove aside the images of the ferocious sea monsters that had launched themselves onto the ship and attacked his friend.

Well . . . his sidekick.

He winced, remembering how Rusty had called him a hero after what he'd done for Brynn.

But that word only forced his thoughts in the direction of his brother, Charlie.

Was he still in a coma?

Had his condition worsened?

And if the darkness in Raven was connected to the darkness everywhere, as the Sage had said, then what impact did Tyler's actions of extinguishing the first flame have on Charlie?

More importantly, could Michael, Brynn, and Rusty really stop Tyler if he was being driven by darkness?

Michael thought back to the moment when he'd seen the strange metallic object form in Tyler's chest and recalled his own struggle with the darkness in Lumina.

Charlie's love and forgiveness had saved Michael.

But Charlie wasn't here.

And Michael was no Charlie.

Maxine's death had driven Tyler mad. To overcome that level of darkness, Michael would need the full power of the light—the energy of a thousand blazing suns. But as Michael examined his crew, their ship, and his own abilities, it felt like the light within him was merely a sputtering flame, a waning ember. He stared out at the open water, wondering how on earth he'd ever outwit Tyler, save Raven, and ultimately rescue his brother.

Rusty interrupted his thoughts. "You're going with me, right?"

"Going where?" Brynn asked.

Michael watched Rusty prepare a rowboat to be lowered into the sea.

"I told Rusty I'd help him bait the queen."

"Bait her?" Brynn stared past him toward the rowboat. "Isn't that what the golden lure is for?"

"Yes, but we need to lead her to it," Michael explained. "Rusty said smaller vessels like rowboats draw less attention from sea dragons. They're more likely to attack ships because ships are more likely to have treasure."

"So wait, you're getting in a rowboat?" she asked incredulously. "In water teeming with sea monsters?"

Michael winced. "Sea dragons."

"Same thing!" She hobbled a step closer. "You can't do that. You're going to get yourself killed!"

"Since when do you care if I live or die?"

Brynn lowered her voice. "Believe it or not, Prince of Lumina, since the moment I saw you at the Sage's cottage."

Michael's eyes widened.

"Don't get me wrong, I hate what you did to Charlie. But I've never hated you. I disliked you strongly for a time—"

"Isn't that the same thing?"

She waved his words away. "I was pretty bitter after you and Charlie left Lumina the first time. After being orphaned and having no family, I couldn't understand how anyone could hate their brother the way you hated Charlie."

Michael stared at his boots.

"I had a lot to process after Charlie left. The Sage helped me work through some of it. But he said forgiveness was a journey I'd ultimately have to take alone." She swallowed. "I like Charlie, you know."

Michael shifted from foot to foot. "You mean you *like him* like him?"

She scoffed. "No. Charlie is like a brother to me." She folded her arms over her chest. "And you felt like the enemy who was stealing my family from me—again."

"I'm sorry, Brynn. I wish I could take it back. All of it. Everything that happened between me and Charlie on the island, what took place in Lumina, and my failure to protect him back at the ranch. I don't deserve to be called Charlie's brother." He sighed. "But I am Charlie's brother. And somehow, his life is once again in my hands. But this time, I'm not fighting him. I'm fighting for him."

Brynn inched closer, dropping her arms. "And so am I." She cleared her throat. "Which is why if you're going to plop yourself down into sea-dragon-infested waters in a dinghy, then I'm going with you."

"Absolutely not," Michael said without hesitation.

Brynn braced her hands on her hips. "Excuse me?"

"Yeah, no," Michael said emphatically. "You almost died, Brynn. Yesterday. Twenty-four hours ago. You can barely walk."

"What about you? You're just a kid. What can you do to help?"

Her words cut him.

Rusty appeared before Michael could say something he'd regret. The sealord wrapped an arm around Michael's shoulder. "He's going with me and Jimmy because he's a hero. Ain't that right, lad?" Rusty winked at Michael. "And apparently, he's the only one on board who can shoot a bow and arrow."

Michael hoped Brynn wasn't thinking about all the arrows he'd shot at Charlie while in Lumina.

Rusty slapped him on the shoulder. "It's time to go, lad. I'll make a sealord out of you yet!"

✦ ✦ ✦

Michael watched the schooner drift away as Rusty and Jimmy tugged on the oars of the small rowboat. The sun descended behind the ship, outlining the crests of the waves with a red-golden glow.

"We need to get at least a hundred yards away from the ship," Rusty said. "Then, Michael, you'll fire an arrow in the direction of the hive."

"With the gold dust, right?" Michael asked for clarification.

"Aye. Here it is." Rusty handed Michael a small drawstring pouch.

He opened it, finding about a teaspoon of gold powder.

"And here's this one." Rusty passed Michael an identical pouch, this one with a palmful of fine golden residue.

"What's this one for?"

The rhythmic dip of the oars slapped the water.

"You'll loosen the strings on the first pouch, loop it over the tip of your arrow, and shoot it into the hive. That'll get the queen's attention. We'll have to move quickly after that. The males will surely wake once their queen is on the move."

"So then what?" Michael asked.

"Then, we pull away as quickly as possible. Jimmy and I will row, and you'll sprinkle that pouch of gold onto the surface of the water, creating a trail back to the ship."

"Back to the ship?"

"Aye, to the trap."

"Right," Michael breathed.

"This is the only way, lad. It's a dangerous task." Rusty lifted his sleeve, revealing a gnarled scar that ran the length of his forearm. "But it can be done."

"So you've killed a queen before?"

"Uh, not exactly . . . But almost."

Michael's stomach flipped.

"So we bait her toward the ship, then lure her into the trap . . ."

"Where she'll be dazzled by the golden lure and rendered less threatening by the copper . . ."

"And then?"

"And then the crew will pull the line that snaps the

trap closed and haul her aboard where we'll cut off her head." Rusty touched the harpoon at his side. "Or stab her though the heart. Those are the only two ways to kill them."

"Excellent," Michael said, his voice dripping with sarcasm. "It all sounds very straightforward. Except the part where we stir up the males because we've trapped their queen. And this time we're in a rowboat that's only slightly longer than the monsters beneath us. No, it all sounds *great*."

"You've got a better idea?"

Jimmy watched them with a curious, unconcerned expression. "Come Monday, everything will be juuust fine."

"What does that mean?" Michael asked.

"Ignore him," Rusty said. "It's just one of his many odd expressions. The man doesn't even know what day of the week it is. He's a fine first mate, but a few sailors short of a crew, if you know what I mean." He tapped the side of his head.

"No, I don't know what you mean," Michael started to say, but Rusty didn't let him continue.

"It's time." He picked up the bow and arrow and handed them to Michael. "Let's hope you have good aim."

With only a slight tremble in his hands, Michael

loosened the drawstring on the pouch to allow the golden contents to fly out upon impact with the water. He looped the pouch over the end of the arrow, nocked it, and pulled back on the bowstring as he'd done countless times back at the ranch during archery practice.

And back in Lumina, when he'd hunted his brother.

He hadn't picked up a bow since then, thankful Mr. Abbott had introduced him to the sport of fencing.

He exhaled slowly through his mouth, releasing a quivering breath, then released the arrow in the direction of the hive. He watched it sail through the sky.

Rusty waited for it to hit the water, then started rowing backward.

"Nice work. Now, sprinkle in the gold dust as we make our way back to the *Penelope*. The lighting is perfect. The setting sun should catch the gold, making it more visible to the queen. She loves a shiny snack."

"I hope we're not her snack," Michael said while shaking bits of gold dust over the side of the rowboat. "How'll we know if we've caught her attention?"

"We watch for her spines. The razor-tipped points on the backs of the males blend in with their blue color. The females' spines are golden, a side effect of eating the mineral. It reacts with the toxin in their blood to create the color."

"So she's poisonous too?"

"Aye. More than the males. But as I said, it takes much more to provoke her."

Michael saw a glittering line of gold points cresting through the water. He swallowed. "Like how much more?"

Rusty's eyes widened. "There she be," he whispered. A little louder he said, "Pull, Jimmy. We need to reach the ship before she does."

Fifty yards away, the golden spines disappeared beneath the water. She resurfaced closer, gulping gold dust as she swam.

Michael gripped the sides of the rowboat.

"Keep sprinklin' that dust. We need her to follow us straight to the trap."

Several yards behind the queen, the waters began to writhe.

"Uh, Rusty . . . I think we have a problem."

The sealord squinted. "Son of a sailor! The hive is stirring. Pull, Jimmy!"

The gray-haired man heaved against the oars, grunting.

A loud crack echoed over the water.

One of the oarlocks snapped, and Jimmy's right oar splashed into the water.

"Blast!" Rusty doubled his speed, throwing his weight into every pull.

Michael leaned over the edge to grab Jimmy's oar

before it drifted out of reach, then saw a giant dark-blue creature slither beneath their boat. Its tail bumped the hull, jostling them, and the pouch of dust slipped from his hand.

"We're out of gold," Michael said, leaning back from the water. "And I think the males know we're here."

Rusty didn't answer. Sweat beaded his brow. The tip of his tongue stuck out and pressed against his upper lip as he pushed himself to row harder.

Finally they neared the schooner.

"There it is!" Rusty said, rowing past the trap and toward their ship. "We just need to get to the stern so the crew can pull us off the water."

He navigated the rowboat around back and made quick work of attaching the necessary pulleys to lift them. Several crew members peered over the edge, ready to help.

"Tell them to get ready to close the trap!" Rusty shouted.

The crew passed the word down the ship and began raising the rowboat.

Michael kept his eyes trained on the writhing mass in the distance.

Thirty feet from the boat, the water exploded as the queen leapt like a porpoise and smashed her thick body against the trap.

Rusty clutched Michael's arm. "It appears she's hungry."

The crew pulled the trap closer to the ship, shortening their distance to haul her aboard once they'd secured her. The queen's body breached the water again, her golden spines cresting, then disappearing in an undulating wave.

Michael couldn't take his eyes off her.

The trap jerked in the water as she smashed into it again, trying to figure out how to reach the golden lure inside. The crew pulled it even closer. It bobbed beneath the suspended rowboat where Michael watched.

"She's inside!" he shouted to Rusty. "We did it!"

"Close the trap!" Rusty shouted to his crew. The two men who'd been raising the rowboat rushed to help, leaving Michael, Rusty, and Jimmy hovering halfway up the side of the ship.

"I said close the trap!" Rusty shouted again.

But nothing happened.

Michael glanced up to see several crew members heaving on the line.

"It's stuck," he said under his breath as he looked down at the writhing queen, who was clearly visible through the weave in the basket. He peered up again, seeing Brynn among the crew, eyes wide as she undoubtedly recalled her last encounter with a sea dragon.

Before Michael could string together any logical thoughts, he dove off the side of the rowboat and into the cool waters.

The splash and rush of bubbles muffled any shouts from above. Michael opened his eyes and blinked against the blurry blue world. Despite the chaos of trapping the queen, a serene underwater silence enveloped him. He saw the trap straight ahead and the writhing blue and gold monster inside. He kicked toward it, careful to stay on the backside of the trap, away from the opening.

A current rushed behind him, movement like a large sea creature. Adrenaline coursed through his veins as Michael tucked his feet up under his body and grabbed the line, pulling himself toward the stuck door that would seal the queen inside.

She peered up at him through the weave of the basket. Her gold and turquoise eyes locked on Michael. A frill of razor-tipped fins surrounded her reptilian face like a lion's mane. She bared two rows of glistening fangs and released a horrifyingly shrill screech.

Startled, Michael pushed off the trap and surfaced for a gulp of air.

The second his head broke the water, Rusty screamed at him. "Get outta there, lad! You're gonna get yerself killed!"

"I have to shut the trap! I can get it!"

"Didn't you hear that?" Rusty leaned over the side of the suspended rowboat. "She's calling for her hive! I've already seen one of the males. Get outta there while you can!"

"Michael!" Brynn shouted from above, but he couldn't see her. "Get out of the water!"

But Michael sucked in a deep breath and dove beneath the waves, one thing on his mind.

He could do this. He would do it.

For Charlie.

Michael used the line attached to the trap to lower himself directly on top of the basket, then pulled himself around to the opening. He gripped the makeshift lid and yanked on it, trying desperately to snap it closed. The queen spun, her body coiling and uncoiling, her golden spines coming dangerously close to Michael's face.

She writhed as if in pain. The copper wire held her at bay.

Michael yanked again on the trap door, then saw the tangle of white line that prevented it from closing. He'd have to reach in to unravel it.

He thrust his hand inside.

The queen shrieked again.

Michael felt movement behind him.

Below him.

In the distance he saw a blurry wave of dark-blue slither through the water. It undulated past him and kept going—three feet, five, seven . . . The thing was at least twelve feet long.

Michael fumbled with the rope, nearly there.

His lungs burned as the trap door finally budged.

He yanked harder on the knot. It unraveled in his fingertips as the queen's fangs snapped and grazed him. A burning fire seared his hand, then his leg as whip of spines lashed him from behind and sliced through the back of his thigh.

He bit back his scream and gave one final yank on the door.

The trap snapped closed.

Michael's grip on the basket faltered. Red seeping from his body tinged the sea. Swirls of dark-blue beasts thrashed around him.

A splash sounded through the water. A large mass in a threadbare sweater swam toward him, a silvery metal staff in hand. Through the blurry water, Michael thought he saw a glimmer of red hair.

Michael's reflex to breathe spasmed in his chest.

A current of water rushed toward him from below. Pain ripped through his body. He felt suddenly cold, freezing, and yet burning hot at the same time.

Rusty grabbed him by the arm, pulling him through

the water as he jabbed with his harpoon, stabbing a massive male sea dragon. He yanked the weapon from the beast's side and spun, releasing Michael's arm and diving straight toward the caged queen. The last thing Michael saw was the old sealord stabbing his harpoon through the weave in the cage.

A blood-chilling shriek rippled through the ocean. Then Michael blacked out.

✦ ✦ ✦

Michael awoke on the mattress in the captain's quarters. A bandage wrapped his right hand. Another bound his left thigh where the leg of his pants had been cut away. Even both of his feet were bandaged. He tried to turn his head and groaned.

Brynn appeared at his side. "He's awake!" she shouted.

Seconds later Rusty burst through the door, his soaked clothes stained with blood.

"Oh no," Michael mumbled, his voice raspy. "What happened to you?"

"Me?" Rusty glanced down at his clothes. "This is yer blood, lad."

Brynn touched a hand to Michael's forehead. "You almost died."

"Did I?"

She nodded, and Winny peeked over her shoulder to stare at him.

"Rusty had to give you mouth-to-mouth."

Michael winced. "Good thing I was unconscious for that."

Rusty chuckled. "Seems he's going to be just fine." He sighed with relief. "We had to use the last of the antidote on you, the entire jug. But we shouldn't be needin' it anymore."

"The queen?" Michael asked.

"Aye." Rusty's dark-brown eyes glinted. "She'd dead. Along with her hive."

"It was crazy," Brynn said. "The crew and I could see them from above. There were dozens of them and at least a hundred more approaching in the distance. The second Rusty harpooned the queen, they all sank."

"Back to the depths from which they came," Rusty added. "But lad, we never would've got her if not for you."

"You saved us," Brynn said.

"A foolish move," Rusty said. "But heroic." He grinned and reached out a hand. Wrapping his thick fingers around Michael's wrist, he yanked him into a sitting position.

"Ow!"

"Best to get you up and moving. Besides, I want to show you something."

Rusty draped Michael's arm over his shoulder and helped him hobble out onto the main deck.

"It's morning," Michael groaned, blinking against the daylight.

"It's afternoon," Rusty said. "And look."

He pointed to a landmass not even fifty yards away. "That there is our island and the location of the second flame. Jimmy took us toward the shore after we defeated the hive."

Light flickered through a crack in the craggy, mountainous peak in the center of the island.

"We did it," Michael said.

Brynn stood on his opposite side. "No, you did it."

Rusty slapped him a little too hard on the back. "Aye. You did. You're a regular old sealord. Now, c'mon. You've got a riddle to solve."

CHAPTER ELEVEN

Raven

SEVERAL HOURS LATER, Michael, Brynn, and Rusty stood at the helm of the *Penelope*, Rusty guiding their ship around the island once again while the kids stared at the map.

"I'm tellin' ya, lad. There's no way onto this island. It's sheer cliffs all the way around, no beach in sight. Not so much as a foothold to get on it."

"There has to be a way onto the island," Michael said, tapping the map. "This is the location of the second flame."

Rusty scratched his chin through his thick red beard. "I thought so too, but now I'm not so sure."

"But we saw a flickering light," Brynn said. She peered up at the towering landmass and pointed to the rocky mountainlike feature in the center. "Up there."

"Could've been anything," Rusty said. "A trick of the light, a reflective object . . ."

Michael silently read the riddle on the map as the ship rounded one side of the island. They passed a towering waterfall that thundered down the side of the cliff. Misty rainbows sparkled in the sunlight.

Rusty shouted to be heard over the surge of water that pounded the surface of the sea. "We'll finish this lap around the island, then that's it. We'll scour the surrounding area to see if there's any other landmasses."

Brynn elbowed Michael in the ribs.

"Ow. What was that for?"

She leaned toward him and said, "We can't leave. This has to be the location of the second flame. Where else could it be?"

He rubbed his side. "I know."

"Then say something to Rusty."

Michael cleared his throat and spoke up. "It has to be this island, though, right, Rusty? I mean, the sea dragons were protecting it."

The sealord glanced at Michael, then back at the water as he guided the ship. "Well then we've got to figure out another way to get onto the island. I'm open to suggestions, lad."

Michael chewed the inside of his lip, then said, "What if we don't have to get *onto* the island?"

Brynn and Rusty stared at him. Even Winny cocked his head.

Michael read the riddle aloud.
"Through writhing seas you must prevail,
And heavy downpours you must sail
Beyond the queen's ferocious hive,
Bestow her treasure to survive.
Subdue her and the seas shall still,
Permitting those who dare and will
Divide the veil of deepest blue
To find the flame that burns with truth.
Shine, shine, O light, shine,
Through darkness to the flame divine."

"And . . ." Rusty said.

"And there's a thought that's been gnawing at me since we made our first lap around the island."

"Go on," Brynn said.

"Through writhing seas you must prevail," Michael repeated. "That seems to be about the sea dragons."

"Aye."

"And heavy downpours you must sail."

"The storms we ran into," Rusty recalled, referring to the torrent of rain and nearly capsizing waves they'd weathered a few days back.

"But what if that's not what the riddle is talking about." Michael read from the map. "Divide the veil of deepest blue to find the flame that burns with truth."

"Shine, shine, O light, shine," Brynn concluded, her

eyes widening as if she understood. "Through darkness to the flame divine."

Winny squawked. "Follow the light!"

"Exactly," Michael said. "The light we saw was coming from *inside* the cliff. Not on top of it." He sucked in a deep breath, bracing for Rusty's response. "I think we have to sail through the waterfall."

The old sealord lifted his eyebrows. "Through the waterfall?"

Michael nodded. Brynn joined in, fully committed to his crazy idea.

Laughter erupted from Rusty's mouth. He doubled over, then straightened. "Do you know what that waterfall would do to a ship of this size and uh . . . quality? Not to mention, most waterfalls have a cliff behind them. We'd be sailing straight into a rock wall or capsizing our vessel. Neither of which I'm thrilled to do."

Brynn folded her arms over her chest. "What happened to going all in? I thought you bought the field and the pearl?"

"Well, I—"

"That's what I thought," Brynn said. "You're *not* fully committed to this mission."

Rusty squared his body to face her. "Now listen here, lass, you don't know me and what I'm committed to!"

"Then prove it," she said. "You told us you believe in

this mission. More importantly, you said you believe in him." She took a step closer to Michael. "I believe in him."

Rusty shook his head and turned back to the helm, muttering under his breath, "Thank the good Mother Ocean I never got blessed with children." He grumbled, then directed the ship toward the waterfall. "Jimmy!" he shouted. "Rally the crew."

Within minutes all the sailors stood before them.

Rusty cleared his throat. "As your captain, it's important to me that I never force you to risk your lives. It should always be your choice. Michael here believes the flame we seek is inside that rocky landmass and that to reach it, we must sail through the waterfall."

Murmurs drifted through the group.

"We'll put it to a vote. All in favor, raise yer hands."

No one moved.

After several silent beats passed, one of the female sailors spoke up. "Michael, why do you think that?"

He sucked in a nervous breath. "Because of the riddle. It's the only thing that makes sense."

"I don't think your brain makes sense," one of the other sailors mumbled.

The murmurs began again.

"Hey!" Brynn interrupted.

Everyone turned to stare at her.

She pushed loose tendrils of hair from her freshly tanned face. "You don't know Michael very well, but I do." She caught his eye and continued. "What you don't realize is that the world of Raven is under attack by a dark force. Michael has experience with this darkness because he's defeated it once before and saved an entire kingdom. Not only that, but he also helped to save me and his brother, Charlie. And if there's one thing I know about Michael . . ." She held his stare. "It's that he'd do anything for his brother."

Michael swallowed.

"There's not enough time to explain everything, but Michael's brother is in danger, and his life is tied to the fate of Raven. So you can believe that if Michael is motivated to save his brother, he's going to save this kingdom. And if Michael says sailing through the waterfall is how we do it . . ." She straightened her shoulders and lifted her chin. "Then that's how we do it." She hardened her face and scanned the group. "Now, all those in favor?"

No one moved for what felt like minutes. Finally one of the other female sailors said, "Brynn's right. We all saw the way Michael dove in to close the trap on the queen. If he hadn't done that, the hive would've attacked the ship again. And this time, we all would've died." She raised her hand into the air. "It sounds crazy. But I'm with Michael."

Brynn thrust her hand up. "I'm with Michael too."

Several of the other sailors slowly raised their hands.

Rusty nodded, then lifted his. "I'm still with you, lad. But you gotta admit, sailing through a waterfall sounds crazy."

Michael grinned.

Jimmy raised his hand last. "I'm with the captain and the kid."

"Good," Michael said. "Then brace yourselves and set the course for"—he turned and pointed to the thundering blue curtain of water—"there."

It didn't take the crew long to line up the ship with the waterfall. Michael and Brynn tried to stay out of their way, standing near the bow.

"Hey," Michael said. "Thanks for backing me up."

Brynn shrugged. "It was nothing." She stared straight ahead, watching as the tip of the ship neared the roaring sheet of water. "Hey . . . I'm sorry." She turned to face him. "I've been a real jerk."

Michael felt a smile tug at his lips. "Only at first," he said. "And for most of our journey." He laughed.

She chewed her lip. "You saved my life. And then you saved the crew. Rusty is right about you. You're a hero. And I know you're going to save Charlie." She faced the waterfall as the boat pierced the thundering stream. "If we don't die."

"Thanks for the encouragement," Michael said, taking a step closer to her.

Water pummeled the deck. Mist and spray soaked their clothes and hair. If Brynn said something else, Michael couldn't hear it over the thundering roar.

Their shoulders brushed.

The ship lurched and started moving faster as if caught in a current.

Michael could hardly see through this mist.

Adrenaline pulsed through his veins as he wondered if he'd been wrong about the riddle.

A wave of uncertainty coursed through him and settled in his gut. He squinted, feeling the schooner tremble and rock beneath his feet, yielding to the violent water that drew her in.

He glanced at Brynn, who held Winny on one arm, shielding him from the water with her body as best she could.

The ship lurched again.

Michael heard a distant shout from Rusty but couldn't make out a single word above the roaring water. He stumbled on the slippery deck as *The Penelope* careened to one side. It felt like they were going to flip. Without thinking, he reached over and took Brynn's free hand and squeezed.

She squeezed back.

The veil of water parted.

Cheers erupted from the crew as a cavern became visible through the thick mist.

Michael peered up at the divided sheet of water, watching as the foremast of the ship passed through it. "Impossible."

"This entire journey has been impossible," Brynn said.

"Aye." Rusty joined them. "A world of impossible things. You did it, lad." He smacked Michael on the shoulder. "I never doubted you."

Brynn rolled her eyes.

Within a few minutes, the *Penelope* had completely passed through the waterfall. The veil closed behind them, leaving their ship caught in a current that pulled them through the dark cavern.

"Where are we going?" Brynn asked.

Rusty shook his head. "Wherever the sea takes us, I suppose. Let's hope it's leading us toward the light."

Winny shook his body and stretched out his wings, flinging droplets of water into Brynn's face. "Through darkness to the flame divine!"

"Good boy," Brynn said, handing him a piece of soggy dried fruit from her leather pouch.

Michael pointed straight ahead. "I think Winny is right."

Ahead, a subtle blue light pulsed. The current pulled the ship around a bend, never once allowing it to hit the bottom or the sides of the underground river.

"Whoa!" Brynn took a step forward. "Look."

The walls pulsed with turquoise and sapphire-colored light, illuminating a crystal structure that lined every surface of the domed cavern.

"It's beautiful," she uttered.

Michael stepped up to the rail and peered over the side. "The water is glowing too."

Brynn and Rusty joined him.

"Bioluminescence," Rusty explained. "The algae produces light."

"It's stunning," Brynn breathed. "And it looks like it's marking a path."

A line of electric blue curved through the water.

"Follow the light!" Winny chirped.

"Well, we don't have much of a choice now, do we? The current is pulling the ship. And right along this glowing path." Rusty chuckled softly, then his laughter shifted to weeping. He wiped his eyes discreetly, but the old sealord couldn't hide his tears.

"What's wrong?" Brynn said.

Rusty sniffed. "I been searchin' my entire life . . ." His voice cracked.

"For the flames," Michael said.

"Not even that, lad." He wiped his snotty nose on his sleeve. "For somethin' that made me feel alive. Somethin' that gave me hope."

The ship followed the curve around another bend. A brilliant light pierced the cavern.

"Mother Ocean." Rusty dropped to his knees and clutched his chest. "There she is."

Michael and Brynn turned to see an elegant lighthouse made entirely of blue and green sea glass. It soared a hundred feet up, its tip nearly touching the top of the cavern. The crystal walls of the cave reflected the pulsing turquoise hues.

Michael's mouth fell open. A flame flickered through the windows in the top of the lighthouse. His eyes traced a small opening in the crystal ceiling, where the light seeped through to the outside.

"It was worth it," Rusty said.

Michael couldn't look away from the flame. "What was worth it?"

"Sellin' my home and the boatyard." He sniffed. "It was worth it."

"Now what?" Brynn asked.

Michael breathed deeply, feeling a flicker of hope in his chest. Under his breath, he said, "I'm coming, Charlie." Louder he said, "We go ashore and take the flame."

✦ ✦ ✦

Michael, Brynn, Rusty, and Jimmy stood in the center of the small circular room at the top of the light-house. A six-foot-tall tripod sat in the center. A strange metal object nestled in a metal ring at the top, a fiery flame flickering above it, a three-foot-long tongue licking the air. Heat pulsed in the room.

Brynn, Rusty, and Jimmy didn't move, too enraptured by the flame's beauty. But Michael took a step toward it. A sense of awe overwhelmed him.

His mind unleashed memories of standing inside the spire of Lumina, basking in the glow of the light of the world, the brilliant orb that illuminated the entire city.

He placed a hand over his chest, feeling his own heart thunder behind his ribcage, then took another step forward.

"What are you doing?" Brynn asked.

Michael shook his head. "I'm not really sure." Heat engulfed his hand as he reached up to touch the metal object that looked like a bowl holding the flame. His fingers instinctively grazed the bottom of it.

The light flickered from white hot to a pale shade of blue. The heat dispersed, then returned with the flame's white color.

"The bowl isn't hot," he said and carefully lifted the object from its stand.

The flame danced in front of him. Its color returned to blue, and this time it remained. He turned, holding it away from his body. "We have to figure out a way to get it aboard the ship."

"Can you carry it?" Brynn asked.

Michael nodded.

Rusty exchanged glances with Jimmy. "An open flame on the ship isn't my favorite idea. We should take the tripod to secure it."

"Good idea," Brynn said.

"What's this for?" Jimmy asked, reaching for a small key on the side of the bowl.

"Don't!" Michael commanded.

Jimmy jerked away, held up both hands, and stepped back.

"What is it?" Brynn asked.

Michael stared down at the object, realizing it wasn't a bowl at all. In the flickering glow, he could just make out the mechanics. "It looks like there's a seam in the metal . . . and maybe a lid that's retracted inside." He lifted the half sphere to eye level and examined it closer. "I can't be sure, but I think if we turn the key, the lid will close."

"Which would extinguish the flame," Brynn said.

She sighed. "That was close."

"That must be how Tyler did it," Michael said. "But it doesn't make sense. Why would the Divine Flame have a way to extinguish it built right in?"

Winny bobbed his head up and down, then swayed side to side on Brynn's shoulder. "Always a choice."

"He's right," Brynn said. "The Sage says the light always offers a choice."

The hypnotic flicker of the flame transported Michael's mind back to Lumina. "We need to be careful with this. We can't allow anyone to turn this key."

"Good call," Brynn said. "Here, I'll hold it while the three of you disassemble the stand.

Michael started to hand it to her, but as soon as the flame passed from his hands to hers, the color shifted from blue to white.

Brynn screamed and thrust it back into his hands. The flame flickered blue once again.

"It's hot!"

Rusty's eyebrows knit together. "You claim you're no magician," he said to Michael, "but clearly you have powers the rest of us don't. The map responds to you and so does the flame. I'll ensure the crew steers clear of it."

"Now that we have the flame," Brynn asked. "What do we do with it?"

"Good question," Michael said. "I hadn't thought that far."

"I have," Rusty said. "If what you say is true about a dark and dark presence in Raven, then I say we get this flame to the king. He can protect it."

Michael nodded. "Sounds good."

"But it's too valuable," Jimmy protested. "I thought the flames promised treasure beyond our wildest dreams."

"Some treasures don't come in the form of rubies and gold," Rusty said. "This isn't open for discussion. We're taking the flame to the king . . . unless Michael says otherwise. He's the true captain of this mission."

Heat flushed Michael's cheeks. "Rusty is right. We need to protect this flame from the darkness." He thought back to the light of the world in Lumina. "Besides, we can't hoard it. A treasure like this should be available to everyone."

Brynn eyed him curiously. "You've come quite a long way, Prince of Lumina."

"That's Captain Prince of Lumina to you," Rusty said. "Jimmy, help me with this stand." He shook his head. "We need to get it on the ship. And quickly. Before the darkness comes to snuff it out."

✦ ✦ ✦

Despite his deep sense of urgency to flee the island, Rusty insisted the crew spend the night inside the turquoise cave. After mounting the tripod to the deck, he'd said, "I wasn't thinkin' about the fact we'd be sailing out o' here with a giant beacon on our bow. Much as I hate to say it, we'd be best to wait until morning to leave. Otherwise, we'll be spotted immediately."

Both Michael and Brynn had protested, saying they needed to get the flame to the king as quickly as possible. They'd already lost too much time battling the sea dragons. But Rusty assured them they were better off hiding in the cave than sailing through the darkness with a spotlight.

When the light of day finally pierced the veil of the waterfall, the crew made quick work of preparing the *Penelope* for the next leg of her journey.

"You look concerned," Brynn said, coming to join Michael beside the flame near the bow.

He checked and rechecked the fixtures Rusty and Jimmy had constructed to secure the tripod. Heat radiated from the white-hot fire, which seemed to cool only when he touched it.

"I was just thinking, what happens if it gets wet?"

"What? The flame?" she asked.

"Yeah, I mean, we got soaked even though the waterfall parted for us. What if the flame gets wet? Maybe we should tuck it away inside the captain's quarters."

"Absolutely not!" Rusty overheard them and approached. "Look at the height on that thing." The flame flickered at least three feet above its six-foot-tall stand. "The captain's quarters are made entirely of wood. And there's enough whiskey in there to . . ." He paused, laughed, then said, "Well, we'd burn the ship down. Look, lad, this is the safest place for the flame."

Michael swallowed, then nodded.

"Besides," Rusty said, "it seems fitting to keep it on the bow; that way it can lead us. Follow the light. Right?"

Michael's concern melted. "Right."

"Good. Now once outside this cave, we'll set our course for the Isle of Majestas. There we'll find the king."

"Where's that?" Brynn asked.

"I have my map," Michael said, pulling it out. He unrolled it and held it toward Rusty. The sealord froze. A smile curled his lips.

Michael glanced down and saw that new text had appeared on the map. "The coordinates to the third flame."

"Aye. And another riddle."

"What's it say?" Brynn peered over his shoulder.

"No!" Rusty snatched up the map and rolled it. "We mustn't tempt ourselves with the third flame. Not yet. First we must secure this one with the king."

Brynn glanced at Michael. "But now that we know where we can find the third flame, doesn't it seem like a waste of time to take this one to the king first?" She yanked the map from Rusty's hand, unrolled it, and scanned the parchment. "Here's the Isle of Majesta, all way down here." She pointed to the bottom lefthand corner. "Look how far away it is from where we are now. The third flame is much closer than the king. What if Tyler gets there before we're back?" She started to read the riddle, but Rusty took it from her.

"That would be a worry if not for the legends," Rusty said. "The Three Divine Flames are three and yet one. As the story goes, you must possess all three to harness their full power. If we can keep one from your friend, we can limit the damage he can do."

Brynn sighed. "Makes sense, I guess."

"We're in agreement then? To the Isle of Majestas?"

"Yes," Michael said.

Rusty gave a swift nod and began barking orders to the crew who guided the ship along the underground river, which now pulled them out to sea.

Brynn stayed beside Michael near the flame. "You're still worried about it."

He sucked in a shaky breath and nodded, eyes on the looming waterfall.

"I've been thinking," she said. "If the darkness here in Raven is connected to the darkness in Lumina, then wouldn't that mean the light in Raven is the same light we know in Lumina?"

Michael nodded, but kept his eyes trained on the fine mist that engulfed the bow of the ship.

"And what do you know of the light in Lumina?" Brynn said.

Thundering water hit the deck, encroaching on the flickering flame.

Brynn reached over and squeezed his hand. "Light can only be hidden," she said, "never destroyed."

Michael held his breath.

"No matter what happens next, even if the waterfall extinguishes the flame, the story isn't over. Just like it wasn't over in Lumina."

He could barely hear her over the roar of the water.

She stepped closer, threading her arm through his as they watched the curtain of water draw near.

Seconds before it engulfed the flame, the waterfall parted.

The crew burst into laughter and cheers. Michael exhaled. And the *Penelope* sailed through to the other side. He turned to watch the waterfall close behind them.

Brynn's grip on his arm tightened. "Uh, Michael?"

With a grin he couldn't contain, he faced her. "We did it!"

Her body stiffened.

"What?" he asked.

She pointed.

A clipper approached.

Pristine white sails.

Dark hull.

And a fluttering flag featuring a black flower.

Michael glimpsed the flame, feeling the warmth of its heat, hoping Brynn was right, that the flame could never be destroyed.

Because even though he had no proof, he knew Tyler was aboard that ship.

And Michael was certain, if Tyler got a hold of the flame, he'd do everything in his power to destroy it.

CHAPTER TWELVE

Earth

SARAH SAT BESIDE MILO in the main entertainment room at the villa. Scientists, military personnel, and even the villa staff gathered around, all eyes fixed on the giant television screen. A deeply unsettled feeling sat heavy in Sarah's gut. She'd felt it since the night before, when Mr. Abbott had discussed with her and Milo the president's decision about the Anomaly. She swallowed and tucked her hands under her legs.

History unfolded before her eyes as two newscasters appeared on the screen above a red bar with the words *Live News Coverage*.

"Thank you for joining us today, America," the female news anchor said, "as we tune into live coverage of the strange phenomenon the world is calling the Anomaly..."

The woman's words faded from Sarah's awareness as the screen transitioned from the image of the news anchors to a live shot of the dome. Dozens of ships bobbed in the ocean, much farther back than Sarah had seen them when she and Milo were last on the water.

She leaned forward, resting her elbows on her knees, trying to discern if the dome was actually larger or only appeared that way. In the two days since they returned from the White House, Sarah had overhead more than one conversation among the scientists discussing the Anomaly's rate of growth. From what she understood, the size hadn't changed significantly, but it was enough to cause concern—and to cause the president to decide to take drastic action.

She swallowed against the building nausea.

The camera panned over the Gulf of Mexico, capturing the blue waters and the swirling gray mass. She squinted, trying to see the island through the churning clouds and electric jolts.

"As you can see," the male news anchor's voice narrated, "all watercraft and aircraft have been ordered to stay out of the blast zone."

Sarah's chest tightened. Her stomach clenched. Just as it had when Mr. Abbott told her and Milo about the president's decision to fire missiles at the Anomaly.

Both she and Milo had vehemently insisted that Mr. Abbott call the president and tell him not to go forward with the plan. With tears in his eyes, he told the children he'd already done so.

"But he said we're like family!" Sarah had shouted through sobs.

Mr. Abbott had remained composed, though redness ringed his eyes. "I know," he said. "But he's also the president of the United States. He has an entire nation to consider—and the world."

"How could he do this?" Sarah had screamed, her voice shrill and cracking. "We met with him! We told him everything he wanted to know! He promised to do everything in his power to help us!"

"He is. But the dome is nearly five times its original size now and showing no signs of slowing. It could easily destroy anything it encounters. The world is screaming for a solution."

Milo had remained unsettlingly silent through the entire conversation.

Sarah's stomach churned, empty because she'd skipped breakfast, too sick to even think about food. Milo leaned closer and took her hand in his. He released a shaky breath. Sarah had never seen him nervous before. Never seen him scared. The look on his face threatened to unravel her last thread of composure.

A wave of rage swelled inside her as she listened to the news anchors describe the unfolding events with nonchalant detachment.

Little did they know that there might very well be two boys trapped inside that dome.

She squeezed Milo's hand and turned to him. "What do we do now, hero?" she asked.

When he looked at her, tears pooled in his eyes. "I—I don't know."

His admission shook her. More than Mr. Abbott's. More than the president's.

Seeing unflappable Milo at a loss stripped her of any remaining hope.

"The movie is over, isn't it?" she whispered.

He didn't say anything, just set his jaw and turned back to face the television screen.

The banter between the two news anchors ceased. Three triangular jets appeared on the screen, flying in formation.

Bile edged up the back of Sarah's throat. "I can't watch," she said, lowering her gaze to her lap. "Tell me when it's over."

A set of hands landed on Sarah's shoulders. She didn't have to look to know it was Mr. Abbott.

"It appears the first missile has been fired," the female anchor said.

The room fell eerily silent.

Sarah held her breath. Seconds passed like centuries as she waited.

A collective gasp erupted.

"Look!" Milo said.

Drawing on every ounce of strength she had, Sarah dragged her gaze up to look at the television screen. A spiderweb of lightning danced violently on one spot of the dome, looking like a shattered windowpane where a baseball had crashed.

The mass of cloud and storm writhed around the puncture wound.

But no explosion followed.

"What happened?" Sarah asked.

"It absorbed the missile," Milo said. "Look! They fired another one."

And another.

A total of six missiles pierced the dome, three rounds of two. With each attack, the storm clouds of the dome raged with menace and flared with lightning.

But nothing else happened.

Eventually the storm and light show subsided. The camera tracked the three jets as they retreated.

"It appears the attempts to destroy the Anomaly didn't succeed," the female news anchor stated. "We'll continue our live news coverage and report any changes as we learn of them."

Chatter filled the villa's entertainment room as the group dispersed. Sarah picked up snippets of technical jargon from two naval officers chatting behind her and a couple of theories from the scientists in the room. She tuned out their voices, eyes trained on the television screen that everyone else had abandoned.

The words of the benefactor glided through her mind.

"You can't fight fear with fear," Sarah whispered. "We must choose another way."

A chill slithered down her spine, her arms. Goosebumps dotted her flesh, and the hair on the back of her neck stood at attention.

"We just attacked it out of fear," she said under her breath.

Something about the appearance of the dome had changed, but Sarah couldn't put her finger on it. A deep sense of dread pulsed through her body.

She pulled herself up from the sofa and stood in front of the television, watching the watercraft return to the invisible boundary that existed a half mile off the dome—the barrier only she and Milo had penetrated.

The news anchors reported. "Looks like the military and research vessels will continue monitoring the Anomaly . . ."

Milo came to stand beside Sarah, but no one else in the room gave the news coverage an ounce of their attention, many of them returning to their work in the makeshift labs and offices they'd set up on the private island.

Sarah squinted at the dome. "Something's different," she said to Milo. "I can't put my finger on it."

"It's spinning," he said. "Look." He tapped the screen. "The clouds moved randomly before, but now they're all going in the same direction."

"That's it." Sarah followed the wisps of gray as they moved clockwise under the dome.

"Sarah." Milo gripped her arm and pointed.

"Oh my—"

The naval vessel that had been the first to reach the half mile boundary crossed the invisible threshold.

"Folks I don't know if you're seeing this," the male news anchor said as the camera zoomed in on the ship. "The naval vessel on your screens just crossed the barrier . . ."

The room fell silent once again as everyone turned their attention to the television.

"The water is moving," Sarah said to Milo. She stiffened. "It's moving really fast."

The naval vessel bounced on the waves, racing toward the Anomaly until the circling current pushed it off course.

The waters churned like a whirlpool.

Someone gasped behind Sarah.

The camera zoomed in. A man in uniform appeared on the deck of the vessel, then jumped overboard. Another followed.

Their heads appeared through the waves as they desperately tried to swim away from their ship.

The camera panned out. The other vessels on the water turned and began to steam in the opposite direction.

The room had fallen so silent that everyone heard Sarah as she quietly stated, "It's growing."

The dome expanded.

A man in uniform stepped closer to the screen, then said, "Someone get a chopper out there! We need to pull those men from the water."

The dome encroached on the naval vessel. The ship that belonged to the nation's military appeared as nothing more than a toy boat swirling around a bathtub drain.

"You can't fight fear with fear," Sarah said to Milo.

The dome swallowed the naval ship, then the two men who'd desperately tried to outswim it.

The waters churned violently, faster.

And faster.

The dome raced toward every other ship on the water.

Sarah knew they'd never outrun it.

Chapter Twelve

She tuned out the voices of the news anchors and the panicked chatter of military personnel and scientists as they fled the room.

"You were right," she said to Milo. "We did make the island angry. And now it's furious."

CHAPTER THIRTEEN

Raven

THE *BLACK DAHLIA* SLICED THROUGH the water, racing toward the island and the second eternal flame, which Tyler could see flickering on the bow of a ragged schooner straight ahead.

He knew in his bones it was Michael.

He'd known it the instant he saw the ship sail impossibly through the waterfall, finally illuminating the meaning of the riddle he'd been trying to solve during their three-day journey from Isla Sordes.

Tyler smiled to himself, silently thanking Michael for making the task of securing the second flame so easy.

Tomlin appeared at his side.

"Do you have cannons on this ship, Admiral?"

A wicked grin spread across Tomlin's face. "Of course I do."

Tyler folded his arms over his chest, not even

needing the voice of the Prince of Chaos to tell him what to do next.

He pointed straight ahead. "Blow that ship out of the water."

✦ ✦ ✦

The black-hulled clipper carved through the sapphire waves, headed straight for the *Penelope*, then cut a wide turn, exposing her starboard side.

A chill crystalized in Michael's veins.

Rusty's gruff voice bellowed over the fading roar of the waterfall, but Michael couldn't process the words, too horrified at the thought of losing the second flame.

The gunport hatches along the sides of the *Black Dahlia* rose in unison as a couple dozen cannons peeked out.

Brynn shouted Michael's name, tugging desperately on his arm.

But he couldn't move.

Couldn't breathe.

This couldn't be happening.

Rusty's words finally penetrated as the old sealord shouted, "Get down!"

Wood crackled and splintered.

The *Penelope* careened, throwing Michael and Brynn to the deck.

Rusty barked orders. The crew ran back and forth across the ship, several descending to the gun deck to prepare a counterattack.

Before Michael could even get to his feet, another cannon smashed into the side of their ship.

The schooner lurched forward, dipping bow-first at a horrifying angle.

"The flame!" Michael shouted, finding his voice.

Brynn grabbed his arm and gasped.

The tripod remained rooted to the deck, but the metal bowl jostled in the ring that held it. The flame danced wildly.

The third cannonball hit. The *Penelope* shuddered, and the flame's housing bounced from the stand, over the edge, and into the sea.

✦ ✦ ✦

Tyler watched as the current pushed Michael's ship closer to the *Black Dahlia*. The *Penelope* leaned at an impossible angle, taking on water, and daring to throw her entire crew into the depths. Tyler's heart raced as he witnessed the flame fly over the edge of the deck and into the deep-blue waters.

Get it! the Prince of Chaos commanded.

Without hesitation, Tyler slipped off his shoes, climbed onto the rail, and dove.

A roar of bubbles greeted him, then faded. The sounds of muffled chaos reached him even below the waves. He swam for the surface and flicked his hair from his eyes.

Not even fifty yards away, the hemisphere that held the flame floated on the waves. Fire flickered above it, and the water surrounding it bubbled in a rolling boil.

He glimpsed Michael on the deck of the battered ship, crouching beside a red-haired girl, trying but failing to get his feet under him as another cannon grazed their vessel.

Hurry! Before Michael gets to it!

Tyler twisted in the water to face his ship, where Tomlin watched calmly from the top deck.

"Throw me a line!" Tyler yelled.

He didn't have to be fast, just faster than Michael.

And Tyler *was* fast.

He tied the line around his waist and took off in a freestyle stroke, covering the distance to the flame in under thirty seconds.

He barely had time to wonder how the metal bowl could possibly float before he reached it. The temperature of the water shifted from cool to warm to burning.

What are you waiting for? Get it!

Tyler tuned out the noise: the shouts of Michael's crew, the boom of cannons.

He winced at the boiling water, sucked in a deep breath, and dove beneath the waves, hoping what he'd learned in science class about hot water being less dense than cold was true.

The temperature dropped as he sank. Grateful for the relief, he opened his eyes and peered up at the surface, able to see the bobbing metal bowl. Though his vision blurred underwater, he could still make out the key in the side. He swam upward, making a slow ascent, hand first.

On the first try, his fingers grasped the key. Screaming at the boiling heat, he turned it.

A loud click sounded under the waves. The water instantly cooled, and the metal orb started falling.

Tyler's fingers locked around it before it sank into the depths. It no longer held any buoyancy. Or a flame.

He kicked upward and broke the surface. "Pull me in!" he shouted to Tomlin.

The two ships drifted closer to one another. Tyler peered up at the damaged schooner, locking stares with Michael.

"Tyler! Don't do this! Please. It's not too late."

The line around Tyler's waist went taut. He rolled onto his back, kicking and clutching the ember to his chest. He could already feel the water begin to swirl around him.

Well done, my ssson. Well done.

His body flew through the water as Tomlin and the crew hauled him back to the *Black Dahlia*, and Tyler shouted back, "It's not too late for me, Michael. But it's too late for you."

✦✦✦

Breath barely filled Michael's lungs. He collapsed against the rail of the ship, watching the ember of the Divine Flame disappear with Tyler as his crew hauled him back aboard.

The *Penelope* lurched, then started moving.

He peered over the sloping bow to see the water begin to swirl.

"Oh no."

He backed away from the rail, screaming for Rusty. "We need to get out of here!"

The *Black Dahlia* turned, her sails full as she raced away from the island.

"Brynn!" he screamed. But he couldn't see her. She'd disappeared during the attack.

Sailors rushed the deck, trying to do what they could, but the tug of the whirlpool was already too great. It whipped the ship around the landmass.

Then faster, bashing the hull against one of the island's rocky cliffs.

A few hundred yards off the island, the ocean erupted. A massive, clouded wall rose from the depths of the sea.

"No," Michael whispered. "No, no, no."

The whirlpool whipped them around the island again, providing a final glimpse of the *Black Dahlia*'s sails over the rising barricade.

Tyler had made it out with the flame.

Again.

The wall towered and tilted, forming a solid dome. The storm and ocean stilled, darkening to a familiar black glass-like sea.

They were stranded.

Again.

And this time, their ship was sinking.

CHAPTER FOURTEEN

Earth

SARAH AND MILO SAT on the ends of their beds, staring out the windowed door to their room's private balcony. Pandemonium had broken out after the news coverage of the growing dome, and Mr. Abbott had ordered the children to stay put and to stay out of the way.

Through the open door that led to the hallway, they'd seen countless men and women rushing past. White coats swished by with each frantic scientist. Heavy footfalls echoed down the corridor as military officials strode from one end of the villa to the other.

She glanced at the clock. Nearly four hours had passed since they'd witnessed the violent whirlpool form around the dome. Thankfully no other vessels or humans had been swallowed by the angry Anomaly. But Sarah couldn't shake the image of the boat caught in the flow and those poor men overcome by the current.

She wrung her hands, recalling what she'd overheard one of the scientists say before Mr. Abbott had ordered them to their room: at the rate the dome was expanding, it would reach their private island in just two days. Maybe sooner.

Heels clicked in the hallway, then stopped. Sarah recognized a female voice—one of the scientists.

"We just analyzed the latest feedback from the probes," the woman said, voice tight.

"Go on," a male voice responded.

Sarah craned her neck. She couldn't see the speakers but identified the male voice as the lieutenant who'd questioned her and Milo after they'd broken through the barrier and touched the dome.

"The Anomaly has been expanding at steady but slow rate. Not anymore."

"Elaborate."

"An hour ago, the dome began growing exponentially. It's moving fast. Much faster."

The lieutenant swore under his breath. "How much time do we have?" His voice faded with the click of the scientist's heels.

"Less than . . ." But that was all Sarah could hear.

She jumped off the end of the bed, her heart in her throat. She strode past Milo, who'd buried his nose in a book—one of Michael's. She flung open the balcony doors and stepped outside, drawing deep breaths of the salty ocean air.

Gentle waves lapped at the beach. She scanned the blue waters. In another situation, the view would've captured her attention. But focusing on the beauty of the landscape seemed pointless when there was a chance it would be swallowed up in a day or two.

"Much faster," she whispered into the wind, trying to shake the scientist's words. But she couldn't blot them from her memory.

Milo joined her, leaning his forearms on the rail. He said nothing, allowing his presence to communicate what words couldn't.

A series of large waves crashed against the shore. The rhythmic sound soothed Sarah's anxious mind. She fixed her eyes on the line that split the sky and sea, watching whitecaps roll and race into shore. They grew larger with each trough and crest.

Wind whipped the balcony, flinging strands of Sarah's short black hair into her face. The sea roared with crashing waves. Gray clouds formed on the horizon.

"Looks like a storm is rolling in," Milo said absently.

The temperature dropped. Water droplets spattered their faces. But when Sarah peered up at the sky, not a single cloud obscured the sun. She wiped a finger against her cheek, then touched the water to her tongue.

"It's salty," she said.

Milo shrugged.

"It's salty," she repeated. "It's not rainwater."

Milo tested the droplets. "Then what is it?"

A rumble sounded in the distance. A buzz of energy caused her skin to tingle.

Sarah jumped as a massive wave crashed against the shore. "It's ocean water."

Droplets continued to spatter their faces as the kids watched a ten-foot tall wave beat the beach, followed by two more that dwarfed the first.

The storm clouds pressed in, a distinct swirling pattern emerging.

Sarah grabbed Milo's forearm. "Look!"

Beneath their feet, the balcony rumbled.

She could just see the faint outline of the dome on the distant horizon. Like a tidal wave approaching them. The salty mist was coming from the expanding dome!

Sarah backed away from the rail, dragging Milo with her into their room.

"Milo! Sarah!" Mr. Abbott's frantic voice boomed behind them. He raced into the room and grabbed them both by the shoulders. "We need to leave," he said. "Now. We're evacuating the island."

The Journey Continues

BOOK SIX
TREASURE BEYOND WORLD'S END

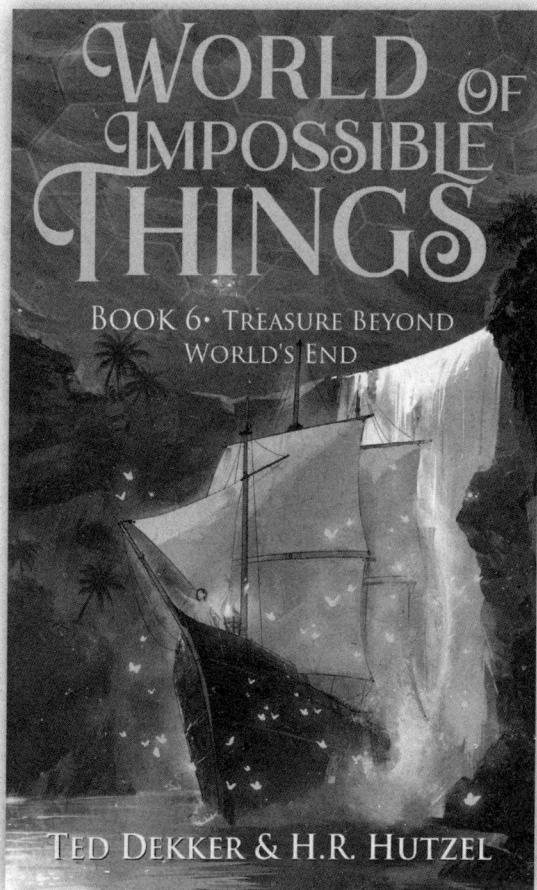

MORE ADVENTURES AWAIT

THE IMPOSSIBLE PLACES SERIES

Journey to Impossible Places

World of Impossible Things

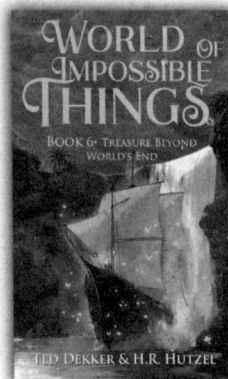

Discover the entire
Dekker young reader universe.

THE DRAGONS SERIES

And They Found Dragons

Dragons Among Us

THE DREAM TRAVELERS SERIES

The Dream Travelers Quest

The Dream Travelers Game

THE MILLIE MAVEN SERIES

WWW.TEDDEKKER.COM